The Time Travelers

The Time Travelers

Meet Some of the Women Who Paved the Way for Equal Rights in California

by Steve and Susie Swatt
and Jeff Raimundo

SUNACUMEN
PRESS
PALM SPRINGS, CA

Published in 2020 by Sunacumen Press, Palm Springs, CA
Produced in conjunction with The Friends of California Archives

The Time Travelers contains fictional accounts
of real people and events from California's rich political history.

Library of Congress Control Number: 2020909866
Publisher's Cataloging-In-Publication Data
(Prepared by The Donohue Group, Inc.)
Names: Swatt, Steve, author. | Swatt, Susie, author. | Raimundo, Jeff,
author.
Title: The time travelers : meet some of the women who paved the way for
equal rights in California / by Steve and Susie Swatt and Jeff Raimundo.
Description: Palm Springs, CA : Sunacumen Press, 2020. | Summary:
"Mrs. Johnson's class travels back in time to interview California women
who fought for suffrage, equal rights for women and minorities, better
schools, the environment, workers' rights, and political opportunity"--
Provided by publisher. | Interest age level: 012-016.
Identifiers: ISBN 9781734564310
Subjects: LCSH: Women--Political activity--California--Juvenile fiction.
| Women--Suffrage--California--Juvenile fiction. | Suffragists--Califor-
nia--Juvenile fiction. | Feminists--California--Juvenile fiction. | Women
social reformers--California--Juvenile fiction. | CYAC: Women--Political
activity--California--Fiction. | Women--Suffrage--California--Fiction. |
Suffragists--California--Fiction. | Feminists--California--Fiction. | Wom-
en social reformers--California--Fiction. | LCGFT: Historical fiction.
Classification: LCC PS3619.W395 Ti 2020 | DDC 813/.6--dc23

Illustrations and cover art by Sandy Bradley
Cover design and interior formatting by
Sunacumen Press
Set in Adobe Minion Pro, Calibri and Chalkduster

ISBN: 978-1-7345643-1-0
Printed in the U.S.A.

Table of Contents

To Learn More

A Note
from the Authors

The Friends of California Archives, a nonprofit organization, was created to promote the use of historical records and illuminate research possibilities that are housed in the multitude of archival facilities in institutions that share our goal of keeping history alive and helping make the link between the past, present and future.

This book would not have been possible without the leadership and assistance of Caren Daniels Lagomarsino, president of The Friends of California Archives. She devoted her lengthy career in the California Secretary of State's office to expanding the public's participation in our government.

We would also like to acknowledge the help of educators Robin Taylor, Sarah Kirby-Gonzalez, Marni Gunlach; Lorie Shelley, California State Senate Photographer; California State Archives; and Greg Lucas, California State Librarian.

This book was a labor of love to educate children about trailblazing women who broke barriers and created opportunities for California females. We recognize we could not identify everyone.

To share additional stories of remarkable women, or offer feedback on this book, please send us an email to: thefriendsofcaarchives@gmail.com.

Dedication

Growing up with my mother, I had no idea she was such a groundbreaker. I never dreamed she'd become a trailblazer for women and Asian Americans. But I did know she was a principled, hard-working, determined, and smart woman who did not let obstacles of birth or circumstance block her way.

I am pleased and proud that this book has been written—partly with funds from my late mother, former Secretary of State March Fong Eu. She would be humbled to be included in its pages as well, although there is no doubt that she belongs there. Her history of firsts is remarkable—the first Asian-American woman to lead the American Dental Hygienists Association, to serve on the Alameda County Board of Education, to be elected to the State Assembly, to earn the votes to become California's Secretary of State, among others.

I am especially excited about this book because it opens eyes to the many often-unrecognized accomplishments and efforts of women to bring equality to our laws, society, culture, and economy throughout this state's history. That children will read its pages and learn about these remarkable women is a

Dedication

wonderful opportunity that my mother, a life-long educator, would love.

—*Suyin Stein, daughter of the late Secretary of State and Ambassador March Fong Eu*

Foreword

California became a state on September 9, 1850. At that time, California had a non-native population of about 100,000, and almost all were men who had come to the new state during the Gold Rush. The women had few rights. Under the state's first Constitution, they were allowed to own property, but they could not vote and had very little chance to work at regular jobs and earn money. Over the next 170 years, women worked hard to get rid of these barriers and to increase women's rights.

They became important role models for current and future generations of women. Beyond that, these risk-takers overturned social, political and cultural barriers—benefiting all Californians and helping to make the state what it is today.

Introduction

Nicole, Caleb, and Lupe were best friends and were so excited to return to school after their summer vacation. Mrs. Johnson was going to be their teacher. She was well known for the way she taught, which made learning in her classes fun, exciting, and different.

As they entered the classroom, they saw a picture that had been taped to the whiteboard.

"What is that?" Nicole whispered in Lupe's ear. Lupe couldn't hear her. She was watching a video on her phone.

Caleb recognized the drawing immediately. "I think I know what that is," he said. "It looks like a time machine. Look, it has a screen that says 'Date' and 'Location.'"

"OK, students, quiet down. Good morning and welcome back to school everyone. You know the rules. Please turn off your phones and take your seats," Mrs. Johnson said. "This year, we will be doing something very exciting and different."

The teacher pointed to the picture on the whiteboard. "This is a brand new invention—a time machine."

Some of the students gasped. One mumbled, "I don't believe it. That's bull!"

1

Introduction

"It's real, and it works," the teacher said. "This year we are going to focus on the contributions that women have made in California history, going back even before 1850, when California first became a state. Besides reading about these women, we'll also be making trips in the time machine so we can actually meet the women we're learning about. Everyone will get to go on a trip—including the boys, who need to learn about these women too."

"Are you kidding?" shouted Malik. "I can't wait to take a trip in a time machine. That'll be so cool."

The students started shouting at once:

"When do we start?"

"Who is going to be in the first group?"

"Does it hurt to travel through time?"

Donald raised his hand. "I'm not sure I believe all this. You can't build a time machine. How come I've never heard of it before?"

Mrs. Johnson told the students that the time machine was a new invention built by a team at the University of California in Berkeley. She explained that her older sister, Valerie, was a scientist who led the team. Valerie had named the machine Alberta, after the famous scientist, Albert Einstein.

"It's really quite amazing," Mrs. Johnson said. "I've already taken one trip on Alberta. We went to Los Angeles in 1955 right after Disneyland opened."

The children were excited.

"Here is my plan," Mrs. Johnson said. "I am going to assign each of you one or two women to research before your time machine trip. Once you return, all of you will write a summary of who you met and what you learned. Karen Olson, the editor of our local newspaper, the *Gazette*, has agreed to publish those stories after our trips are done."

Mrs. Johnson handed out permission slips for their parents or guardians to sign.

"These forms must be returned before you can take a trip on Alberta. It doesn't cost anything, and no one has to go, but I'm sure you will all want to have the experience."

The students were so excited. They wanted to start their research right away.

1

Overcoming Discrimination

The big day finally arrived. Everything was in place. It was noisy in the classroom because all of the students were talking at once.

"Settle down, everyone," Mrs. Johnson said. In front of the classroom—still taped to the whiteboard—was the picture of Alberta, which was made to look like something out of the past so it wouldn't scare the women they were going to study. It looked like a large silver can with big windows and an antenna sticking out of its top, even though it was a modern invention. Mrs. Johnson introduced her sister Valerie, who told the children all about Alberta and warned them about what buttons not to touch. She said Alberta had a new super computer that allowed the time travelers to pinpoint exactly where and when they would land.

Valerie explained that she and her fellow scientists had been working 15 years to create the time machine. She said that after every setback and disappointment, they pledged to keep trying until Alberta worked perfectly. "It was very upsetting when something went wrong," she said, "but we knew we had to keep pushing."

She explained that the students wouldn't feel anything when they went back in time. But she cautioned that they could stay only one hour in each place before they had to go somewhere else or return home. She didn't say why, which only added to the mystery.

In the back of the class, Ms. Olson, the newspaper editor, watched in amazement as she wrote in her notebook, while a photographer took pictures of the entire class.

Mrs. Johnson then called on the first group of time travelers—Amy, Caleb, and Greg—to describe the early women pioneers they would be visiting.

Amy told the class about Biddy Mason, who had been born into slavery in Georgia, but later won her freedom in California. She made a lot of money and helped African Americans and other poor people in Los Angeles. Caleb talked about Mary Ellen Pleasant, who also had been a slave before coming to California. She stood up for her rights in San Francisco in the 1860s and paid for shelter and jobs for escaped slaves in the southern states. Greg said the group also would be visiting a woman named Mary Tape, who fought school leaders who wouldn't allow her daughter and other Chinese-American children to go to their public schools.

After their presentation, Mrs. Johnson explained how hard it was for African Americans, Asian Americans, Native Americans, Hispanics, and other minorities to live in California after it became a state in 1850. She said that the state outlawed slavery. But for many years, escaped slaves who came to California were returned to their owners. She told the students how many Native Americans were killed for no reason at all, and that for a time the Chinese weren't even allowed to live in California.

"Things changed slowly," Mrs. Johnson said, "but keep

6

all of this in mind when you hear the stories of Biddy Mason, Mary Ellen Pleasant, and Mary Tape. They were very brave women who stood up for their rights."

After introducing the class to their substitute teacher, Mrs. Johnson, Valerie, and the students left school for the science laboratory and the time machine.

Once they arrived at the lab, Mrs. Johnson, Valerie, Greg, Caleb, and Amy took their seats inside the machine and strapped on their seat belts. The students gazed at the keyboard and dials with wonder.

"Is everybody ready?" Valerie asked.

The children were a little nervous. Amy chewed on her fingernails. Greg looked around cautiously. Caleb, his eyes opened wide, didn't move at all.

"I'm kind of scared," Amy said nervously.

"Me, too," said Greg.

"Don't worry," Valerie said. "You won't even know you're going back in time, and it'll only take a couple of seconds."

Valerie entered some codes into Alberta's computer. First the door gently shut. Then, the children could hear a whizzing sound and a *whoosh* that startled them. After that, it seemed like Alberta was floating in air for a couple of seconds.

"OK, everyone," Valerie said. "We're here. Los Angeles in 1884." The door opened and everyone walked out. "Remember," Valerie said, "we can only stay for an hour."

"And also remember," said Mrs. Johnson, "take your notebooks and recorders."

Alberta had taken the adventurers to a piece of land on South Spring Street in the busy and fast-growing downtown area of the city. There they were greeted by Biddy Mason, who had owned the property years earlier.

Shortly after the Gold Rush, an enslaved woman named Biddy Mason won her freedom in the California courts and later became a rich busi- nesswoman in Los Angeles. She built the city's first African-American church and the first school for Black children.

Mrs. Johnson told Miss Mason about the school project and the students started the interview.

"How did you get from the South to California?" Amy asked.

"Well," Miss Mason said, "I was born 66 years ago to a family that had been slaves. When I was a girl about your age, I was taken from my family and sold to the owner of another plantation. In 1848, my owner decided to move to Utah, and then to San Bernardino in Southern California. I had to walk 2,000 miles behind his wagon. We arrived in California in 1851."

"Were you freed when you came to California?" Amy asked.

"Not at first," Miss Mason replied. "Even though slavery was outlawed in California, my owner refused to let me or my daughters be free. So, I went to court to gain our freedom. African Americans weren't even allowed to testify against white people in those days, but we won!"

"What happened next?" asked Caleb.

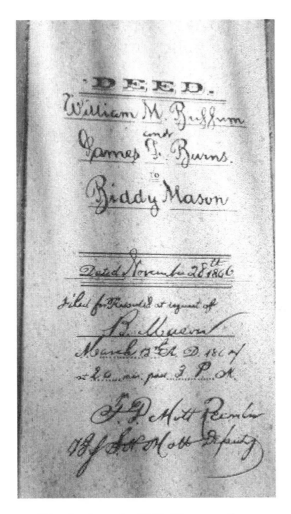

This is a copy of the deed naming Biddy Mason as the owner of a large piece of property in Los Angeles in 1866. It was very unusual for a woman of color to own property in those days.

"We all moved from San Bernardino to Los Angeles," Miss Mason responded. "It was a really small town back then— only a couple thousand people lived here. I was a nurse and a midwife. Do you know what a midwife is?"

"Yeah, I know," said Amy. "You were like a doctor who helped deliver babies."

"That's right." Miss Mason explained that many people hired her. "I saved as much money as I could. When I had saved $250, I bought a large piece of land right here on South Spring Street. Remember, Los Angeles was really small at that time. A businessman offered me a lot of money for the land, and then I bought and sold even more property." She chuckled: "You know I made a lot of money doing that." The children laughed as well.

Miss Mason told the students how she used her property as an orphanage for children who had no parents and as a meeting spot for the city's first church for African Americans. She told them how she helped the poor of all races and built the first school in Los Angeles for Black children.

Mrs. Johnson looked at her watch. "OK, kids, it's time to get back to Alberta." She turned to Miss Mason, thanked her for talking to the students, and said: "You have no way of knowing this now, but in about a hundred years, this piece of property will sit in the middle of a huge thriving city with millions of people. And you'll be happy to know that there also will be a little park in the middle of the property dedicated to you and your good work for the people of Los Angeles."

"Thank you for telling me that," Miss Mason said. "I have tried to live my life doing what's right and helping those less lucky than I."

With just a few minutes left, the group got back to Alberta. Valerie looked in her manual, and then punched the

Mary Ellen Pleasant, who was born into slavery, was a wealthy businesswoman in San Francisco who helped pay for the fight against slavery in the 1850s.

keyboard on Alberta's computer. The upper right-hand corner of the computer screen read: "Montgomery Street, San Francisco, 1868."

Once Alberta's metal door opened, the students found themselves on a busy street corner.

"You must be the children in Mrs. Johnson's class," a woman said. "I recognize you because your clothes are much different than ours. I'm Mary Ellen Pleasant. I've been waiting for you," she said with a smile. "Thanks for coming to hear my story."

Mrs. Pleasant explained that she, too, had once been enslaved. She had come to San Francisco in 1852, because she heard California had outlawed slavery. But runaway slaves could still be caught, so she pretended to be white. She was able to fool people because she had light-colored skin. The city only had about 40,000 people back then, drawn to California by the chance to find gold in the hills. San Francisco was pretty rough. It had drinking and gambling and plenty of people breaking laws.

"I was pretty smart," she said with a twinkle in her eye. "I became a cook in a boardinghouse for rich men, and I used to listen in on their conversations. Oh my, did I get a lot of good ideas that way."

Mrs. Pleasant told about how she'd overhear the men talk about how they made money in the stock market. She saved the money she earned and the money she had been left by her second husband. She invested it in Wells Fargo Bank, gold mines, dairies, and laundries. Pretty soon she was rich and owned several businesses.

"In my research, I've read that you did some wonderful things with your money," Caleb said.

"Well, have you heard of John Brown?" she asked.

"Sure," Greg said. "He was a white guy who fought slavery before the Civil War."

Mary Ellen Pleasant lived in this large mansion in San Francisco.

Mary Ellen Pleasant sued a San Francisco railroad company and forced it to allow African Americans to ride in its horse-drawn streetcars.

"That's right," Mrs. Pleasant responded. "I gave him $30,000 to help him start the fight. I'm very proud of that. I also helped slaves escape and find jobs."

"I understand you fought a streetcar company. Could you tell us about that?" Caleb asked.

"Well, that's pretty interesting," she replied, "and it's good timing because just this morning I won a big case in the California Supreme Court. It all started two years ago, in 1866."

She explained how she and two Black friends—right there on Montgomery Street—were told they couldn't ride in the car because of the color of their skin. "I took the streetcar company to court and won. Streetcars can no longer refuse service to non-whites."

"Wow, what a story," Caleb said. "I can't wait to tell the class."

With that, the group thanked Mrs. Pleasant for her time,

and they moved on to their final stop, also in San Francisco.

This time Alberta was programmed to send the time travelers to Chinatown in San Francisco in 1885. There, standing in front of a small school, called the Chinese Primary School, they were greeted by Mary Tape, a Chinese-American photographer and painter, and one of her daughters, nine-year-old Mamie.

"Hello, Mrs. Tape," Greg said. "We're school students who have come here from the future to learn about how you made history in San Francisco."

"It's nice to meet you," Mrs. Tape said, as she looked at her daughter, "but I'm afraid I haven't changed things as much as I would have liked. You see, there is so much dislike for Chinese people here. It's very upsetting."

Caleb took some notes. "You fought the school system, didn't you?" he asked.

"Yes, I did. Last year, when Mamie was eight years old, I tried to enroll her in our neighborhood public school, the Spring Valley Primary School. Even though California had a law saying all children had a right to public education, the school's principal said Mamie couldn't go. In fact, no Chinese children were allowed to attend."

"Why was the principal against you?" asked Amy.

"Many people hated us Chinese and said some very nasty things about us," Mrs. Tape replied. "We looked different and had different ways of life and religious beliefs. They blamed us for taking away their jobs. Mamie's father and I had come to the United States as children and didn't think this was fair. So we challenged the board of education in court, and we won. The judge said it was not right for us to be banned from public schools that we pay taxes to support."

Mrs. Tape continued, "But instead of letting Mamie into

14

Mary Tape, shown here with her family, fought to give Chinese-American children in San Francisco the right to attend public schools.

Spring Valley, they decided to build what they called a 'separate but equal school'—just for the Chinese children—here in Chinatown. The only problem was that the Chinese school wasn't as good as the white school, and I wanted Mamie and my other children to get good quality educations. Earlier this year, when I went to enroll Mamie in the Chinese school, it wasn't open yet, so I tried again to get Mamie into Spring Valley. And again, they said 'no,' this time claiming that her health records weren't up to date."

"In my research, I came across a letter you wrote in a San Francisco newspaper," Greg said. "Boy, were you mad."

"Yes, I was very angry," Mrs. Tape replied. She then pulled a yellowing news article out of her purse. "I still carry it with me," she said, and she read part of her letter. "I see that you are going to make all sorts of excuses to keep my child

15

out of the public schools. Is it a disgrace to be born a Chinese? Didn't God make us all!" She said she was glad the newspaper printed her letter on the front page. Mrs. Tape then explained that once the Chinese Primary School opened, Mamie and her brother Frank became its first pupils.

With time running out on their visit, Mrs. Johnson told Mrs. Tape about something in the future—that her fight for equality in education finally would be won in California in the 1940s. And, finally in 1954, the U.S. Supreme Court would ban "separate but equal" schools throughout the nation.

"Well imagine that," Mrs. Tape said with pride. "Look what I started. Thank you for telling me that."

"No," Mrs. Johnson said, "Thank *you* for having the courage to stand up for what's right."

Amy, Caleb, and Greg had notebooks full of stories and recordings of their interviews. They couldn't wait to tell their classmates about the three brave women who overcame tremendous obstacles and helped change California.

Supreme Court Decision in a Chinese Test Case.

San Francisco, March 3d.—The Supreme Court to-day rendered a decision in the Chinese test case of Tape vs. Hurley, in which Judge Maguire recently maintained that Mamie Tape, a native of California, but of Chinese parentage, was entitled to admission into the public schools. The

In 1885, Mary Tape won a court case that kept San Francisco schools from banning Chinese-American students.

How Did California Get Its Name?

California gets its name from a book written in Spain more than 500 years ago.

An author named Garcia Ordonez de Montalvo wrote several books about knights and romance. One of them told about a mysterious island paradise called California.

He wrote that the island was near the Garden of Eden. It had steep cliffs, rocky shores, and it was full of pearls and gold. Only large, strong, and beautiful Black women, called Amazons, lived there. These women tamed and rode wild beasts around the island and had gold weapons. Their ruler—Queen Califia—was very beautiful and brave.

In later years, Spanish explorers who remembered the story landed in what is now Baja California and thought it was the island in his book. So they named it California.

2

New Opportunities for Women

As one might guess, news of the time travelers caused excitement at school. Before the morning bell rang, students crowded outside Mrs. Johnson's class and peeked through the windows to catch a look at the picture of Alberta taped to the whiteboard. They clapped when Amy, Caleb, and Greg walked through the door.

"OK, everyone, settle down," Mrs. Johnson said. "We have work to do, and today I'm taking Lupe, Addison, and Vivian with me back to San Francisco in 1881 to meet two more inspiring women who fought hard for equal rights. Vivian, do you want to explain?"

"Yes, we're going to visit Clara Shortridge Foltz and Laura de Force Gordon. Most Californians don't know who they were, but they were really famous back then. Together, they fought job discrimination and worked hard to convince the men to let women vote."

"Alright, then," Mrs. Johnson said. "We're on our way."

The trip back in time went as smoothly as the first one. Alberta sent the students, Mrs. Johnson, and Valerie to a restaurant across the street from the San Francisco courthouse.

There, Mrs. Foltz and Mrs. Gordon were waiting for them, and everyone went inside for lunch.

"I think this is a great class project," Mrs. Foltz told the students. "People often forget history as time goes on. I don't understand how you got here, but I'm sure there are a lot of things about the future that I wouldn't understand."

Mrs. Foltz handed the students a newspaper. There was an article about a sensational murder trial in which she was a lawyer for the prosecution, and Mrs. Gordon was a lawyer representing the accused killer. Newspapers loved to write about that case, especially because it was argued by two women lawyers, which was very unusual.

"How did the two of you come to be lawyers against each other on this case?" Lupe asked.

Clara Foltz of San Jose led the fight in 1878 to end the law that kept women from becoming lawyers. She became the state's first female attorney.

Laura de Force Gordon, the first woman in the U.S. to run a daily newspaper, was California's second female attorney.

"It's a long story," Mrs. Gordon responded. She looked at Mrs. Foltz and said, "Actually it's two long stories."

Mrs. Foltz went first.

"It really started a few years ago when I was living in San Jose. My husband abandoned me and our five little children. He just ran away to Oregon and never came back."

"Oh my," exclaimed Addison. "That must have been horrible for you."

"It was," Mrs. Foltz said. "That was just a few years ago, in 1875. I was 26 years old. My oldest child was nine and my baby was two. I really needed to work so I could feed my family, but the only job I could get was sewing dresses and making hats. I didn't make very much money doing that. I really wanted to become a lawyer like my father, but California didn't allow women to be lawyers."

She explained that for women to become lawyers, the law had to be changed. "So, how did you do that?" Lupe asked.

"Well, the first step was to convince those who write the laws —the legislators at the Capitol in Sacramento—to approve

Senate Bill 66 to allow women to become lawyers was approved by the Legislature in 1878. It was signed into law by Governor William Irwin.
(California State Archives)

the change. Laura de Force Gordon and I worked together to make it happen."

Mrs. Gordon added, "At that time, I was the first female to run a daily newspaper in the entire country. It was called the *Stockton Daily Leader*. But I, too, wanted to be a lawyer, so I helped my friend Clara. It was very hard work. Only men were in the Legislature, and a lot of them didn't like the idea of women becoming lawyers. We had to convince them to do the right thing. We begged and argued for their votes. Eventually, we got them."

"Hooray for you!" Vivian blurted out.

Mrs. Gordon smiled. "But the fight wasn't over. And it

MRS. FOLTZ VICTORIOUS.

Judge Morrison Decides That Ladies May Enjoy the Advantages of the Hastings Law School.

Clara Foltz and Laura de Force Gordon won their lawsuit against San Francisco's Hastings Law School and forced the school to admit women.

was Clara who really saved the day." She turned to her friend. "Tell them what happened next."

"Well," Mrs. Foltz told the students, who were quickly writing in their notebooks, "it takes more than the Legislature to create a new law. California's Governor also has to agree. And the Governor at the time hadn't made up his mind. I was standing outside the Governor's office late one night as he was deciding what to do. Suddenly, someone shouted that the Governor didn't like the idea of letting women practice law."

"Oh no!" the students said in unison.

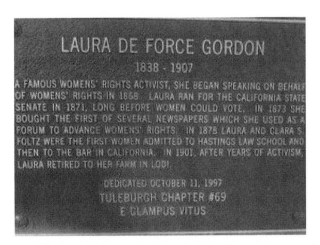

In Laura de Force Gordon's home county of San Joaquin, a plaque commemorates her life-long fight for women's rights.

The Criminal Justice Center in Los Angeles is named after pioneering women's activist Clara Foltz.

"I was very angry and upset when I heard that," Mrs. Foltz said. "It wasn't fair that men could become lawyers, but women could not. So I snuck into his office when the guard wasn't looking and started talking to the Governor face to face. I was pretty nervous, but I told him how important it was for women to be allowed to be lawyers. And you know what? He listened to me and changed his mind—right there on the spot."

"My goodness," said Lupe. "No wonder you're famous."

The women explained that they then wanted to go to the University of California's new law school. "We actually went to classes for three days," Mrs. Gordon explained, "but they kicked us out and told us that women weren't allowed."

"Why?" asked Addison.

"They said women were too much of a distraction for the male students," she replied.

"So what did you do about that?" asked Vivian. "You should have taken them to court!"

"That's exactly what we did," Mrs. Gordon said with a

24

smile. "We argued the case ourselves and won."

Mrs. Foltz was the first woman in California history to become a lawyer and the first woman in the country to become a deputy district attorney, the person who starts legal actions against criminals at the county level. Mrs. Gordon was the second female lawyer in the state.

From their research, the students knew that both women worked hard to convince the men in California to let women vote. In fact, Laura de Force Gordon had given the first public speech about equal voting rights—what was called "women's suffrage" back in 1868—and dedicated much of her life to the

After a successful career as a lawyer, Clara Foltz became the publisher of this women's magazine. In 1930, she ran for Governor of California but lost.

cause. Clara Foltz also became what was called a "suffragist"—someone who supported votes for women. She later owned a newspaper called the *San Diego Daily Bee* and a magazine, *The New American Woman.*

After thanking the two women for their time and congratulating them on their many successes, the students, along with Mrs. Johnson and Valerie, headed back to Alberta and the trip home.

"I'm really sad," Lupe said.

"Why is that?" asked Addison.

"I read some stories about Laura de Force Gordon on the internet before our trip," Lupe answered. "She wanted voting rights for women so much. She traveled all over giving speeches about it. She was a real warrior. But she didn't live to see the day when women finally were given the right to vote in 1911, because she died in 1907—four years before it happened."

What Jobs Did Women Have in the Late 1800s?

For most of the late 1800s, married women were expected to stay at home to take care of the house and children. In fact, most women believed that marriage was more important than working at a job outside the home. And most jobs that did exist for women were for very low pay.

Many of the working women in the late 1800s had jobs as "domestic servants," or housekeepers. Sometimes, they were hired just to take care of children of wealthy families. Other popular jobs for women were working in laundries and factories and making dresses. For many years, most of the teachers were men, but as the number of schools expanded in the years after the Gold Rush, and as colleges started letting women in, many women became teachers. Women also had jobs on farms, picking and sorting fruit.

As California cities grew, women were hired to be office typists. And when department stores were built in many of the bigger cities, young unmarried women were able to get jobs as clerks and saleswomen. It was hard work with long hours, but women simply didn't have the choice of getting the better, higher-paying jobs.

Gradually, laws and customs changed. Women started attending colleges and universities, which prepared them for jobs and professions—from teaching and writing to medicine and law.

3

The Uphill Climb to Winning the Vote

Nicole, Courtney, and Eli strapped themselves into the University of California's time machine, Alberta. They weren't nervous at all, because six of their classmates had told them what to expect.

"You won't feel a thing," Vivian had told them.

Valerie entered the codes on Alberta's computer. A large screen on the console flashed "San Francisco, November 6, 1896."

The students were one of two groups in the class assigned to learn about how California women fought to be allowed to vote. It was called "women's suffrage." Their assignment dealt with the disappointing election of 1896, in which the suffragists fell 26,000 votes short of winning. It was hard to find information about the election in the history books, but they found some stories on the internet. Why did the women lose? Did they learn any lessons that would help them in the future? They had plenty of questions for the women they would meet from the past.

Shortly before the time machine started its journey, Mrs. Johnson turned to the students. "Now remember, unlike the previous trips we've made in Alberta, this time you don't exactly know who you are going to interview. But trust me, you'll have lots of chances to meet some famous women who fought for voting rights. That's why your research work was so important."

Alberta took the students to a spot outside a big auditorium called Golden Gate Hall, where women suffragists —determined to win the vote for California women—were holding a big meeting.

Wait a minute," Eli said. "It's November 6th—that was three days after the election. They've already lost the vote."

Just then, they heard a bunch of boys standing on the street corner shouting. One yelled, "Read all about it in the *Examiner.* Suffragists say they won't give up the fight!"

Another shouted, "Get your *Chronicle* here! All the latest news!"

"Who are those guys?" asked Nicole.

"My grandpa told me about them," Eli said. "He called

Shortly after California's male voters refused to allow women to vote in 1896, a story in the *San Francisco Examiner* told how female activists were planning to continue the fight and were sure of victory.

The nation's most famous women's rights activist, Susan B. Anthony, worked hard on California's unsuccessful 1896 suffrage campaign.

them paper boys. They sell newspapers on street corners. Let's get one."

Eli reached into his pocket and brought out a nickel. He handed it to one of the boys, who looked at it curiously and gave him a newspaper. Eli looked over the pages and saw a story about women holding a big meeting, called a convention, to discuss what they were going to do after they had lost their voting-rights election.

Nicole was the first student to realize that Alberta had dropped them off right in front of the women's meeting. There were hundreds of women. They wore long white dresses with colorful sashes. Many of them carried signs supporting women's right to vote.

Courtney pointed to one woman who had just finished speaking to the crowd. She reminded her of her grandmother. She had gray hair pulled into a bun in the back of her head. "That's Susan B. Anthony. I'd recognize her anywhere. Let's go talk to her."

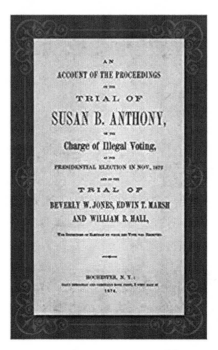

AN
ACCOUNT OF THE PROCEEDINGS
ON THE
TRIAL OF
SUSAN B. ANTHONY,
ON THE
Charge of Illegal Voting,
AT THE
PRESIDENTIAL ELECTION IN NOV., 1872
AND ON THE
TRIAL OF
BEVERLY W. JONES, EDWIN T. MARSH
AND WILLIAM B. HALL,

ROCHESTER, N. Y.:
1874.

In 1872, Susan B. Anthony was arrested for voting in the presidential election.

In preparing for the trip, the students learned all about Miss Anthony and her long fight to give women the vote. Back in 1872, she even broke the law and voted in a New York election. She was arrested and fined $100.

The students pushed their way to the front of the auditorium. They cornered Miss Anthony, explained who they were, and started asking questions.

"Wait a minute," Miss Anthony said. "You're time travelers? That's hard for me to believe." The students did their best to describe Alberta and the fact they had arrived from more than 120 years in the future.

"That sounds crazy. I'm not sure I believe you," she said, "but you certainly don't dress like today's boys and girls."

She pointed at Eli.

"Your shirt says 'Golden State Warriors.' What does that mean?"

Eli explained that the Warriors were a basketball team, but since the game of basketball had only been invented a couple years earlier, Miss Anthony had never heard of it.

"I'm sorry, but we're in a bit of a hurry," Nicole said. "Can we ask you some questions for a school project?"

"Of course you can," Miss Anthony said.

"Well, first of all, were you in charge of the suffrage campaign?" asked Nicole.

"Yes, I was one of the leaders," Miss Anthony replied. "Even though I'm 76 years old, I was brought here from the East to help lead the drive to give California women the vote. I helped get newspapers on our side, and I traveled up and down the state speaking and writing about the importance of women's suffrage."

Courtney then asked, "Why was it so important for women to vote?"

"Oh my, there are so many reasons," Miss Anthony answered. "For one, since women must obey all the laws, we should have a voice in making those laws, don't you think? And since we pay taxes, we should have a vote on the amount of the tax and how that tax money will be spent. It's only fair."

She continued. "Another reason is that women want and deserve laws about morals, education and how people treat one another fairly and with respect—such as giving women equal property rights as men and making mothers equal

"The true republic: men, their rights and nothing more; women, their rights and nothing less."

— Susan B. Anthony

guardians of their children with the fathers. If women had the vote, we could make those important changes in the law."

Eli asked, "The election to give women the vote was just a couple days ago and you lost. Why do you think that happened?"

"Well," Miss Anthony said, "some people still don't think we women are smart enough to vote. Of course, that's poppycock! These are the same people who complain about corruption in government. Who do you think those crooks are and who put them in office in the first place? The men!"

Miss Anthony continued. "But the real reason we lost is because of a sneak attack against us by the California liquor industry. Ten days before the election, the liquor men sent out notices to bars, taverns, and restaurants that scared voters— only men, of course—into believing that women would try to outlaw beer, wine, and liquor if we were given the vote. It frightened a lot of men in this state, and they voted against us."

She paused before continuing. "Still, I really believe that California voters soon will do the right thing and give us political equality. We just have to do a better job of convincing the men of this state."

Just then, Courtney noticed an African-American woman standing by herself in the back of the auditorium. "I bet that's Naomi Anderson. I read about her in a newspaper. It called her, 'a colored lady orator.' Let's go talk to her."

The students thanked Miss Anthony and ran to introduce themselves and their project to Mrs. Anderson.

"I know you had an important job during the election campaign," Courtney said. "Can you tell us about yourself and how you worked to get women the vote?"

"I sure can," Mrs. Anderson said. "I was born in Indiana to free Black parents. Out in the Midwest, I gave a lot of speeches

During the 1896 campaign, Naomi Anderson traveled to Black neighborhoods and churches to try to convince African-American men to vote for women's suffrage.

on the importance of women's suffrage. Last year, I moved to California. All the suffrage campaign leaders were white women, and they didn't let Black women join their suffrage groups. That's called segregation. But I went to many Black neighborhoods and churches and tried to convince Black men to vote for us. I tried to talk to as many former slaves as possible and told them that women would always feel like slaves until they were allowed to vote."

Mrs. Johnson had to cut short the interview. "Good for you for carrying that important message. I'm sorry, but we only have a few minutes left," she said to Mrs. Anderson and turned to the students. "If you want to talk to anyone else, you'll have to be quick."

Ellen Sargent, the president of the California Suffrage Association, had just stepped off the auditorium stage. She received a standing ovation. The students rushed to meet her before she walked away. They knew she was a famous suffragist. And so was her husband, until he died in 1887. Aaron Sargent

THEY WANT SUFFRAGE.

A Few of the Determined Women Who Are Fighting for Recognition by the Democracy.

ELLEN C. SARGENT.

Ellen Clark Sargent of Nevada City and her husband, U.S. Senator Aaron Sargent, were famous figures in the 19th Century women's suffrage movement.

had been a U.S. Senator and member of the U.S. House of Representatives from California for many years, and every year he tried—but failed—to get a bill passed in Congress that would have given the vote to every woman in the nation—not just in one state.

Ellen Sargent was friends with Susan B. Anthony and played an important role in the suffrage movement.

"Mrs. Sargent," Nicole said, "you just lost the big election, but you don't seem to be too upset about it."

Mrs. Sargent paused a second and looked at the hundreds of women in the audience. "These women are ready to try again. We'll rest a little while, then re-start our efforts to get the vote."

"So you're not discouraged, even though you lost?" Eli asked.

"Sure, we're disappointed, but we don't feel discouraged at all. We received more than 100,000 votes from male voters here in California, and most of the newspapers were on our side. You'll see. We'll come back stronger than ever. We'll win eventually."

The students, who originally thought the women would be sad after their election loss, left the auditorium impressed by the encouraging interviews. From their research, they also knew that the women would have to wait another 15 years before California women would finally be allowed to vote.

1896 Election Results
State of California

**137,099 (55.4%) voters opposed
women's suffrage**

**110,355 (44.6%) voters supported
women's suffrage**

Who was Mary McHenry Keith?

A newspaper once wrote about Mary McHenry Keith as "a dainty little blue-eyed, rosy woman." She may have been small, but she played a big, important role in California women's fight for voting rights.

Her father was a judge and didn't approve of women working outside of the home. But he didn't stand in his daughter's way when she wanted to go to college. In 1879, Mary McHenry Keith became one of the first women to graduate from the University of California.

Then, she became the first woman to graduate from the Hastings School of Law after Clara Foltz and Laura de Force Gordon forced the school to let women attend. After practicing law for a few years, Mrs. Keith decided to turn her attention to the fight for women's voting rights.

After the women lost the statewide vote in 1896, Mrs. Keith was a one-woman dynamo. She gave frequent speeches and tried to persuade state lawmakers to give women voting rights. She raised money for the cause and her inspiring talks helped recruit many new members for suffrage clubs.

During the successful 1911 campaign, she wrote a weekly newspaper column and used a new invention—radio—to send messages to listeners urging them to support women's voting rights.

After women finally won the right to vote, Mary McHenry Keith decided to take on a new cause, spending much of the rest of her life pushing for caring treatment of animals.

4

Hooray!
We Won the Vote!

Mrs. Johnson's students were all abuzz after hearing about the women's failure to win the vote in 1896. Nicole, Courtney, and Eli had reported on their interviews and the disappointment of the hard-working suffragists.

"I don't think that was very fair of the people to vote against the women," Carlos said. "Everybody should have the right to vote."

Before she turned her class over to the substitute teacher, Mrs. Johnson wrote on the whiteboard: Wyoming, 1869; Colorado, 1893; Utah, 1896; Idaho, 1896; Washington, 1910.

"These are the states that let women vote before California did," she noted. "Look at Wyoming. It wasn't even a state yet in 1869, but it was the first to let women vote. And do you know one of the important reasons why?"

She waited a few seconds to see if any of the students had an answer. When none raised a hand, she said, "Well, back then, there were very few women living in Wyoming, and the men were lonely. They thought that if they gave them the right to vote, women would want to move to Wyoming and settle down."

Mrs. Johnson told the children that after 1896, California women kept trying to win the vote for 15 years, but elected officials always came up with ways to keep it from happening. "One Governor even had promised the women that he would be on their side, but he later said he was only joking. But everything changed in 1911, because a new Governor and a new Legislature had taken over."

Mrs. Johnson explained that the new leaders—called Progressives—wanted to give more power to the people to run the government—the power to write their own laws and to kick people out of office if they were doing a bad job. They also wanted to give the voters another chance to approve women's suffrage.

"And that's where Keisha, Santiago, Kane, and I are going next in our time machine: 1911. We'll report back what we learn."

They met Valerie at the lab, went through their pre-trip routine, and settled in their seats. Sitting in front of the control panel, Valerie entered the code on the keyboard, turned to the children and smiled. "I think you're going to like this." The big

Campaign posters in 1911 urged California voters (all men) to make the state the sixth in the U.S. to give women the vote.

Suffragists used a fancy new car, called the Blue Liner, to carry women campaigners around the state and to attract the attention of men.

screen said: "335 Powell Street, September 26, 1911."

The time travelers were deposited in front of the famous St. Francis Hotel, across the street from Union Square. It was noisy, with street cars clanging every few minutes. Hundreds of busy San Franciscans walked right past them.

"What are we doing here?" asked Keisha.

"You'll see," Mrs. Johnson said.

A woman saw the students and rushed over.

"Hi," she said, "I was expecting you. My name is Ida Finney Mackrille, and I'm working on the voting-rights campaign." She pointed to a big, fancy car that was parked near the hotel's entrance. "And this is the Blue Liner."

Mrs. Mackrille explained that they were in the middle of another campaign to give women the vote, and that the election was only two weeks away. "We've been having all sorts of problems getting the men to listen to our speeches about why it's so important to let us vote," she said. "We have tried giving talks in big auditoriums, but usually it's only women who show up. But women can't vote, so that doesn't do us much good."

"What does that have to do with the Blue Liner?" Keisha asked.

"Well, cars are pretty new and exciting here in 1911. And the Blue Liner is the fanciest car on the road. It's a 1910 Packard Touring Car. It seats seven people, the top goes down, and it's really expensive."

"How much did it cost?" asked Kane.

"A little more than $4,000," Mrs. Mackrille answered. "In the future, I'm sure cars will cost a lot more than that, but $4,000 today is about seven or eight times more than most Californians earn in an entire year."

"I'm still confused," Keisha said. "How does this help with the upcoming election?"

"Just watch," she said. Within a few minutes, dozens of

Hundreds of California newspapers supported the campaign to give women the vote. In this *Sacramento Bee* cartoon, a man is wondering, "Why shouldn't my mother vote?"

Women formed dozens of special suffrage clubs throughout California to help campaign for voting rights.

men stopped to admire the car. They looked at the tires and the engine. They felt the soft seats. Men walking across the street saw the crowd growing and went to see what the fuss was all about.

Just then, a young boy with a bugle tooted his horn, and that attracted even more attention. Pretty soon, the crowd spilled onto the street, blocking traffic.

Over the noise, Mrs. Mackrille started talking. "Gentlemen," she said, "my name is Ida Finney Mackrille, and I want to explain to you why the women of California need your support at the election in two weeks."

For several minutes, San Francisco voters heard her try to convince them to support her cause. "We work and pay taxes, just like you. We should have the same voting rights you have. It's the democratic and fair thing to do. Some people say women aren't smart enough to vote. I say we are fully able to understand politics. After all, there are thousands of uneducated men who vote."

Ida Finney Mackrille continued for a few minutes, and then let the men continue to inspect the Blue Liner. She returned to the students.

"Whew! I was pretty nervous. Our voting rights depend on the men in this state."

A young couple had watched her speech in front of the hotel, but the man wasn't impressed. "Come along. We've had enough of that. That woman had better go home to her children, instead of talking on street corners," the husband said.

His wife replied sternly, "She has to do that. She can't make you men listen any other way."

Another man then walked up to Mrs. Mackrille and said, "Madam, as soon as you stood up in that automobile, I said to my friend: I'm for women's suffrage!"

Ida Finney Mackrille explained that she had to leave and take the Blue Liner on another job. "We also use the car to drive speakers to small towns, ranches, factories, and farms throughout the state. We're determined to campaign wherever there are men who vote. Many of the roads are pretty bad, but this is a strong car. In one town with 400 voters, more than 200 men showed up. In Vallejo, we parked the car in front of a cigar store and talked to many men."

Mrs. Mackrille said the Blue Liner would be on a special mission on Election Day, driving many old and poor men to the polls so they can vote. "Many of these men can't walk. Many are blind. Many are dying. But they know how important it is to vote. I think many of them will be on our side."

With that, the Blue Liner pulled out and headed for its next stop. Mrs. Johnson, Valerie, and the students rushed to

VOTES for WOMEN

Don't Fail to Vote YES
on the SUFFRAGE AMENDMENT

on OCTOBER 10

Give the Women of California
a Square Deal

They Want the Ballot

WHY? BECAUSE

Suffrage activists argued that since women obey the laws and pay taxes to support government, they should be represented in that government.

Alberta for their next visit. They would remain in San Francisco and jump ahead to October 12, two days after the election.

As Valerie made all the arrangements for the quick jump forward in time, Santiago thought Valerie might have made a mistake. In preparing for the trip, he had read that Election Day back in 1911 was October 10th—not October 12th.

"Shouldn't we be going back two days earlier?" he asked.

"That's a good point," Mrs. Johnson said. "But there's an important reason Alberta is taking us back when she is. You'll find out in just a few seconds. And remember to bring your jackets."

The door of the time machine closed with a clang, and everyone prepared for their next adventure. In an instant, they felt like they were rocking back and forth. And sure enough, once Alberta's door was opened, everyone noticed they were sailing on the water in the San Francisco Bay.

"Hey, we're on a ferry boat," Kane yelled.

They were on a crowded boat that was returning to San Francisco from across the bay in Berkeley. They were immediately greeted by a woman who looked to be about 50 years old. She wore a big hat and a flowing dress down to her ankles. She also wore a sash and had many ribbons on her dress. The students could tell she was a suffragist. And she was smiling broadly.

"Welcome, welcome," said Selina Solomons. "I'm so happy to meet you to talk about our exciting election."

The ferry boat was full of people heading to work in San Francisco. It was windy and cold as the boat moved through the water, and fog hung over the bay. Everyone went inside to keep warm.

Santiago asked the question that he had thought about on the trip back in time. "We're here to talk about the election to give women the right to vote. But wasn't that two days ago?" he asked.

"Yes, you're absolutely right," Selina Solomons said. "It's

a long story. How much time do you have?"

"Less than an hour," Mrs. Johnson said. Ms. Solomons promised to tell her story quickly.

She told the students that she had come from a pretty famous family in San Francisco. Her great-grandfather was with George Washington when he became the nation's first president. And her father had come to California to look for gold. She said she had spent most of her life trying to win the vote for women and was going to write a book about the election.

"Do you know what happened back in 1896?" she asked the students.

"Yes, of course," Kane replied. "The women lost. It made us sad."

"Well," Ms. Solomons said, "we did some things wrong in that election and tried to do better this time."

"Like what?" Santiago asked.

"Well, we did a better job including more working women in the election campaign—like the girls who work in shops and offices. I started a club here in San Francisco and invited all these girls to come by for a real inexpensive lunch. They learned about the importance of giving women the vote, and then they went back to their shops, offices, and neighborhoods and tried to convince the men to vote for us. We set up women's clubs up and down the state."

Ms. Solomons continued: "We wrote articles for the newspapers, sent women to small towns and farms to give speeches, and even made slide shows to show before movies in the theaters. We also made posters and put them up on street corners and in street cars. We handed out leaflets after church services. Last 4th of July, three women flew in a hot air balloon over a big group of people and dropped papers on everyone

How We Won the Vote in California

By

Selina Solomons

Suffragist leader Selina Solomons wrote the only detailed account about how California women won the vote in 1911.

with a simple message: Women of California need the vote because they obey the laws and pay taxes. They should have something to say about how those laws are made. Also, all the mothers in California are in charge of their homes and children and must be able to protect them."

Santiago returned to his question. "I'm still confused. Why are we here on the ferry two days after the election?"

"Well, on election night, there were hundreds of us women in a big auditorium watching the votes being counted. And we were losing. Badly. Most of the votes against us were coming from San Francisco, the largest city in California. We were really sad. Some of us were crying. Yesterday, I was so upset and disappointed that I took the ferry over to visit my sister in Berkeley. Even though many votes hadn't been counted yet,

I didn't want to think about the election anymore."

She continued. "But when I woke up this morning, they had finally counted the votes from the farmers, ranchers, miners, and other people living in small towns. And we had won! Not by much, but we actually won! I was so excited. I quickly rushed to the ferry boat so I can go to a big celebration in the city later today."

"So that's why we're on the ferry," Santiago said. He turned to Mrs. Johnson. "You knew all along, didn't you?"

"Yes," the teacher said. "You see, I did my homework, too," she said with a smile.

The students, Valerie, and Mrs. Johnson each gave Selina Solomons a big hug and thanked her for all her hard work.

"Oh, don't just thank me," she said. "There were so many of us who worked day and night for many years to earn the right to vote. Their names will go down in history once I

California women vote for President for the first time in 1912.

write my book. We don't have all the rights that men have yet, but we're getting closer."

As Keisha, Santiago, and Kane buckled their seat belts inside the time machine, Mrs. Johnson told the students the rest of the story. "You see, the vote in California was really important. We were only the sixth state to allow women to vote, but it helped convince voters in many other states to do the same. And then, nine years later in 1920, women throughout the entire country got the right to vote."

The students couldn't stop talking about Ida Finney Mackrille and Selina Solomons. Keisha said, "I want to be just like them when I grow up."

Gail Laughlin: A Heroine of Women's Suffrage

Before 1911, many women had worked very hard to win the vote in California. It was a difficult job getting the men to agree with them.

But Gail Laughlin helped save the day.

She had grown up very poor in Maine. She studied hard in school, and she and a boy classmate received awards for having the best grades. The boy got a scholarship to attend Maine's best college, but young Gail only got a medal. She decided to spend the rest of her life fighting for women's equality.

Ms. Laughlin saved enough money from various jobs so she could go to college and attend a law school with 123 men and only three women. She became the first woman lawyer in Maine and discovered that women were being paid less than men doing the same work.

Gail Laughlin was convinced that women needed equal rights—starting with the ability to vote—just like men. So she started to work for an organization that was trying to win suffrage battles throughout the country. She was sent to California to organize what were called suffrage clubs—groups of women who tried to convince the men that allowing women to vote was the right thing to do.

Ms. Laughlin created 52 of these clubs and the women took their case to the newspapers before the 1911 election. It worked. The newspapers wrote stories about the women's arguments, and it turned out that just enough male voters agreed.

After the election, Gail Laughlin wrote the law that allowed California women to serve on juries, and she continued to work for women's rights for another 40 years.

In 1919, she was elected the first President of the National Federation of Business and Professional Women's Clubs, which was the first organization to focus on issues facing working women.

5

California's First Women Lawmakers

Mrs. Johnson walked into her classroom about a minute after the bell rang. She had been at a meeting with other teachers and was running a little late. She expected the students to be noisy and restless. Instead, she was surprised to find all her students already at their desks, and no one was talking. Brandon was standing in front of the class.

"What's this?" she said. "How come it's so quiet? Why is everyone paying attention?"

"I was pretending to be the teacher," Brandon said. "Before we go in the time machine to visit her today, I was telling everyone what I learned about Esto Broughton on the internet."

Mrs. Johnson thanked Brandon for being her helper and wrote four names on the whiteboard: Esto Broughton, Elizabeth Hughes, Grace Dorris, and Anna Saylor.

"OK, Brandon, tell everyone a little about these women."

"Well," Brandon said, "we already learned that women won a big election in 1911 and finally were allowed to vote in California. After that election, lots of women decided they wanted to run for office, just like the men, and go the Capitol in Sacramento to help make our laws. But at first it was really

4 CALIFORNIA WOMEN TO GO TO ASSEMBLY

Three of Them Put Themselves on Record as Favoring the National Prohibition Amendment

Mrs. Saylor, Mrs. Hughes and Miss Broughton Discuss Their Novel Positions in the State

FOUR WOMEN LEGISLATORS TAKE SEATS

For First Time in History of State, Sex Is Represented in Assembly; Each Honored by Speaker

"Pioneers" Are Mrs. Anna L. Saylor, Miss Esto Broughton, Mrs. Grace Dorris, and Mrs. Hughes

San Francisco Examiner, **November 10, 1918 (left) and January 7, 1919**

hard for them. Many of these women didn't know how to run for office and ask people for votes. After all, men had been in charge of California for more than 60 years. They had no women role models."

"And when did that change, Brandon?" asked Mrs. Johnson.

"In 1918, four women—those four listed on the whiteboard—became the very first women to win election to the California State Assembly. I was explaining that there are 120 members in what's called the California Legislature. They write our laws. Forty of them are in the Senate, and 80 are in the Assembly. Before 1918, all of them had been men."

"Thanks, Brandon. Good job," Mrs. Johnson said. "Okay, so here's what's going to happen today. Brandon, Alka, and Carlos will be going with me back to meet these four women. Actually, we're going to talk to them twice. First we will meet them right after they won their elections, and then 20 years later we will talk to them again so they can tell us what they accomplished. I think this is going to be a great trip."

The group hurried off to meet Valerie, who was making some last-minute changes to Alberta. "Everything all right?" Mrs. Johnson asked her sister.

"Oh, sure," Valerie said. "One of our other scientists had used the machine to visit Abraham Lincoln, and I was just updating all the computer codes. We're ready to go. Where are we headed today?"

"Well, we're going to be making two stops," the teacher said. "First, we want to go to the California State Capitol in Sacramento. And the date is January 6, 1919."

"OK," said Valerie. "Everybody strapped in? We're off!"

In an instant the two women and three students were transported to the steps of the Capitol. It was cold and foggy, so everyone hurried into the building and walked up to the second floor where the Assembly was just finishing its first meeting of the year. They were excited to see where the lawmakers worked.

The Assembly was like a big auditorium. There were rows of desks for all the members. Off to the side, and in the back, there were desks for news reporters. Large, fancy lights, called chandeliers, hung from the ceiling. The balcony overlooking the Assembly floor was filled with people who were starting to leave.

"Quick, follow me," Mrs. Johnson said. "We're supposed to meet the four women in the back. Just a few minutes ago they became official Assemblywomen."

Standing near the rear door of the Assembly were the four women, surrounded by many who offered their congratulations. They had made history as the first women elected to serve in the Capitol.

Grace Dorris   Elizabeth Hughes

Anna Saylor   Esto Broughton

The women, along with the school time travelers, moved to a private room a few yards away.

"So, what made you decide to run for office in the first place?" Alka asked.

Grace Dorris answered first. "Actually, it happened by accident. My husband was pretty well-known in Bakersfield, and he was planning to run, but he decided that it was more important for him to be a soldier during World War I. So I ran in his place."

Elizabeth Hughes, who lived farther north in the

Sacramento Valley, said she ran so she could help small schools in little towns.

"Was it fun running for office?" Alka asked.

"It was real hard work," Mrs. Hughes said. "No women had ever won before, and people said I was too weak to be in the Assembly. But I showed them, didn't I?"

Carlos laughed and said, "You sure did. How about you, Mrs. Saylor?"

She answered, "Well, I grew up very poor in Indiana. I saw so many children who didn't know how to read. So I am really interested in helping young students like you become real good readers."

Alka then turned to Esto Broughton. Earlier, Alka had noticed that she seemed quite young and that she had trouble walking. Miss Broughton explained that she almost died when she was a child from a rare disease that made her back bone curve and kept her from growing. "But I studied hard and went to school at the University of California in Berkeley and became a lawyer."

"Berkeley?" Alka asked. "That's where our time machine was invented."

Miss Broughton said that she grew up in Modesto, where there were a lot of farms. "I want to help the farmers get water so that they can grow their crops."

"How have the men been treating you so far?" Carlos asked. "After all, you're the first Assemblywomen in history."

"Actually, they've been pretty good to us," Anna Saylor said. "We thought that maybe there would be some jealousy from the men, but so far they've been very nice. Even the newspapers have been respectful. One paper is going to let me write stories for them on subjects that women care about."

Mrs. Johnson then explained that they had to hurry

First four women in the California Legislature in 1918
(Sunny Mojonnier, Women in California Politics Foundation)

back to the time machine, but she said the students wanted to return and talk to them again after the Assemblywomen had spent time at their new jobs. The women agreed and watched the time travelers leave."

"OK, here's what we're going to do," Mrs. Johnson said. "This is going to be fun. We're going to program Alberta to come back to Sacramento in 1938—that's nearly 20 years in the future. That way, we'll find out what important things these four women were able to do. OK?"

"Yeah, let's do it," Brandon exclaimed.

Valerie went to work programming the machine, and before they could catch their breaths, the group found themselves at the front entrance to the Senator Hotel across the street from the State Capitol. It was July 16, 1938. Many people were walking into the hotel, because there was a big party celebrating the 20th anniversary of the election of the first four women to the Assembly.

The students started walking toward a big couch in the lobby, where they were to meet former Assemblywomen Dorris, Hughes, Saylor, and Broughton once again.

Near the couch was a table with several newspapers piled high. Valerie noticed the front page of one paper that had a picture of a gigantic parade in New York celebrating a man named Howard Hughes. Hughes had just flown an airplane around the world faster than anyone before. It had taken him nearly four days to make the trip.

"Wow," Valerie thought. "People living in 1938 probably have no idea what air and space travel is going to be like in the years ahead."

The time travelers and the four pioneering women met and hugged each other. The students, of course, hadn't changed a bit since their first meeting. But the four women were 20

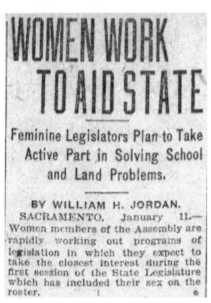

California's first women legislators wrote many important laws about education, equal rights, water, and criminal justice.
San Francisco Examiner, January 12, 1919

years older, and they no longer were in the Assembly. They had other jobs.

"So," Mrs. Johnson said, "the students thought they'd like you to talk about some of your greatest accomplishments when you were in the Assembly. Alka, would you like to go first?"

"Sure, Mrs. Johnson. I'd like to ask Esto, I mean Miss Broughton, if she was able to help the farmers like she wanted."

Miss Broughton smiled. "I think I did a pretty good job. I not only helped them get water for their crops, I changed the law so that farmers could work together to develop electricity for homes and businesses. And, for women, I wrote the law that allows a family's property and belongings to be split between the husband and wife if they get divorced. Before that, the husband didn't have to share it with his wife."

"And what about you, Mrs. Hughes?" asked Brandon.

"Well, like I promised," she said, "I spent most of my time trying to make schools better—especially those in small towns. I was chairwoman of the Assembly's Education Committee, which was a pretty big job. Have you heard of Chico State College? It used to be a small school where people learned how to be teachers. It started in a cherry orchard. But I made sure it received plenty of money so it could grow."

Mrs. Johnson told her that her dream for Chico State would continue because, years later, it would become even bigger, a university.

Grace Dorris told the students that she was responsible for new laws that helped women and poor people. "I wanted to make sure that anyone who is accused of a crime—even someone who has no money—has a lawyer to help them during their trial. And I am really proud to have led the fight that got California to support voting rights for women throughout the entire country—not just in a few states."

Anna Saylor went last. "Right after my election, I visited a prison called San Quentin, near San Francisco. I was really upset at what I saw. Women convicts were in prison there along with the men. They were being held in tiny cells, with no light and hardly any fresh air. I promised that from then on, women would be kept in separate prisons from the men. Later, after I left the Assembly, I worked for the Governor and saw to it that many of the dirty county jails were cleaned up. Do you know that in some of these jails, they kept eight- and nine-year-old children with the grown-ups? And their beds were dirty and covered with bugs."

The teacher gathered the children and started walking to the time machine outside the hotel. She thanked the women for spending so much time with them.

"You four will go down in history for showing girls and women—in fact, everyone—how to succeed when the odds are against them and how to make California a better place," she said. "We'll see to it that you're in the history books."

How Sacramento Became California's Capitol

California has had many capital cities over the years. Monterey served as the capital when Mexico owned California. But after the United States won a war against Mexico in 1848, California belonged to America.

The new California leaders decided that San Jose—about 50 miles south of San Francisco—should be the official capital. But after meeting there for a little over a year, they felt they had made a mistake. San Jose only had some huts, tents, and small adobe buildings for people to live and work in, so it was too small to be the center of government.

The leaders decided to move the capital to Vallejo—to the northeast of San Francisco Bay. But they weren't there for long, either, because there weren't many houses. Legislators had to sleep on a steamboat. And once again, they decided to move the capital somewhere else.

So, in 1853, Benicia became the new capital. Benicia had a nice, big city hall that the new state government used for offices and meetings. But it didn't have enough hotels or boarding houses for the state's leaders to live in.

Finally, in 1854, Sacramento was picked as California's capital. Sacramento was a pretty big city already, because it was the center of business during the Gold Rush. There were hotels and shops, and many of the state's most powerful people lived in Sacramento. In addition, the city was built next to the Sacramento River, which made it easy to move people and goods to San Francisco.

The Legislature met in Sacramento's courthouse for several years, until a new and grand Capitol building was finished in 1869.

6

Women Protect Our Environment

Marina was the first to exit Alberta, the famous time machine. She took one step and gasped.

"Oh my gosh!" she exclaimed. "Quick. Come here. This is amazing."

Her teacher, Mrs. Johnson, knew exactly why Marina was so excited. She smiled and winked at Valerie, and the two of them watched with anticipation as Marina's classmates—Bobby and Luna—stepped out of the machine.

Instantly, Bobby gasped. "I've never seen anything like this before," he said with wonderment.

Marina didn't say anything. She was looking straight up—just staring at a cluster of giant trees. They were so tall, she couldn't even see their tops.

Valerie explained. "We've been transported back to 1933, and we're in a far northern part of California, called Humboldt County. What you are seeing are ancient redwoods, called sequoias. One of the trees around here is about 1,600 years old. And many of them have grown to be more than 350 feet tall."

While Valerie stayed behind to do some work on the

California women's clubs joined together after 1900 to pressure state and local governments to save large groves of ancient redwoods.

time machine, the children and their teacher walked along a neat path that took them through the woods. Everyone was looking up at the big trees.

"This is called the California Federation of Women's Clubs Grove," Mrs. Johnson explained. She pointed to a beautiful four-sided stone fireplace in the middle of a clearing. There were picnic benches nearby. "It's called a hearthstone."

She said the hearthstone, or monument, had just been built by California's first female architect, Julia Morgan, who also designed the famous Hearst Castle along California's central coast. "It's dedicated to the women's clubs, because they helped save these trees from being cut down."

Mrs. Johnson saw an elderly woman sitting on a bench. "Come on, kids, let's go meet Clara Burdette."

"Hi, everyone," Mrs. Burdette said. She looked up at the surrounding giant trees. "Isn't this wonderful?" she said.

Marina replied, "It's amazing. Don't you just love the smell of the trees? And they are so tall I can't even see the sun! We've been reading about you and the job you did to save these redwoods."

"Oh my," Clara Burdette responded. "There were so many women who saved the trees. Not just here, but also the giant redwoods in the Sierra foothills and the Santa Cruz Mountains. But I'm glad I did my part."

"So how did that happen?" Bobby asked.

"Well, many years ago, back in 1900, a number of women's clubs had been formed throughout the state. The women wanted to improve the lives of people who lived in their communities. I created one of those clubs in Los Angeles. But I thought it would be best if all the clubs worked together, so we combined them all into one group—called the California Federation of Women's Clubs. We worked to get the women the right to vote,

Nestled among the giant redwoods in Humboldt County is a monument dedicated to the women who saved the trees from being cut down.

In the early 1900s, large redwoods were cut down to provide lumber for homes and businesses in fast-growing California.

and on specific things our neighborhoods needed."

"And the clubs saved the trees?" Bobby asked.

"Yes we did. We had a big meeting in Los Angeles," Mrs. Burdette continued. "All the clubs were represented. And would you believe it, just four days before the start of that meeting, there was a newspaper article that said a lumber company had bought two huge groves of sequoias in Northern California and was going to chop them down to build houses and other buildings. "

"And you were upset about this?" asked Luna.

"I was," Mrs. Burdette said. "These are majestic trees that have stood for hundreds of years—in some cases, thousands of years. So, when all the clubs joined together, I suggested that we concentrate on three issues—one was getting the vote for women, one was improving the lives of California children, and the third was saving our world-famous redwood trees."

"So, how did you do it?" Luna asked.

"We did lots of things. In our fight to save the trees, we met with President William McKinley. And then when Teddy Roosevelt became President, we sent him petitions with more than a million signatures. He even came here for a visit. We also wrote letters to newspapers and persuaded lawmakers to turn these and other groves into parks. Here in Humboldt County, the fight was particularly difficult."

"Why is that? asked Bobby. "Why wouldn't everybody want to save these beautiful trees?"

"Well, you have to remember that many of the women who lived here were wives, sisters, and daughters of men who worked in the logging business," Clara Burdette said. "People were afraid that these men would lose their jobs if all the trees were protected. Still, many brave women continued to fight to save the trees, and they helped convince the leaders of the county that the trees brought in a lot of tourists, creating many jobs. Women's clubs—and a separate group called the 'Save the Redwoods League'—helped raise money to buy some of the land, and now we're sitting in a state park nearly twice the size of San Francisco."

"Well, Mrs. Burdette," Mrs. Johnson said, "we certainly appreciate you taking the time to tell us all about the redwoods and women's role in saving them."

"It was my pleasure," Clara Burdette said. "I live more than 600 miles away, but I just had to take the train up here to get another look at these magnificent trees. It almost makes me cry to think that I, and so many other women, had a role in protecting these trees forever."

Women Protect Our Environment

**In 1954, members of one men's club wore gas masks during a meeting
to protect themselves from breathing dirty air.**
(*Los Angeles Daily News* negatives [Collection 1387] Library Special Collections,
Charles E. Young Research Library, UCLA)

The children rushed back to the time machine and were anxious to tell Valerie everything they had learned. After hearing their stories, she said, "Okay, is everybody ready? We have one more stop to make before we head back home."

Valerie entered codes on Alberta's computer and set the machine to land in Los Angeles on October 7, 1971. As usual, the time trip took only a split second, and when Alberta's door was opened, the children found themselves on a hill overlooking a busy freeway jammed with thousands of cars. It was late afternoon. There to greet them were two women—Marge Levee and Sabrina Schiller.

"I went to the library and read some old newspapers about you," Bobby said to Mrs. Levee. "They called you a 'smog fighter.'"

68

"Yes that's true," Mrs. Levee said. "Look at the sky here in Los Angeles. It's brown and hazy. That's called smog. It's been this way for many years, and it makes people sick."

Marge Levee explained that smog is caused by many things, especially by cars and trucks that shoot pollutants into the air through their tailpipes. "It's worse here in Los Angeles because we have lots of vehicles and the smog is trapped by surrounding mountains so it has nowhere to escape."

"Maybe you need some giant fans to blow it away," Marina suggested.

"Well, actually, that has been suggested," Mrs. Levee said with a little chuckle. "But the giant fans would require too much energy to use, and they'd be really expensive." Then she let out a bigger laugh. "Someone also suggested that maybe we could shoot huge cannons into the sky to open up holes for the smog to escape. That idea wouldn't work either."

"One of the articles I read said you began fighting smog way back in 1958," Luna noted.

"That's right," Mrs. Levee said. "The smog was getting worse, and it seemed like no one was doing anything about it. I had to take my two-year-old daughter to the hospital because she had breathing problems. So, nine of us women met at our house

As the smog attacks continued in the 1950s, many government leaders failed to act. For many years, they didn't take the smog issue seriously.

Women Protect Our Environment

In 1958, a small group of mothers in Los Angeles formed "Stamp Out Smog," which held colorful rallies to protest government's slow response to the smog attacks.
(Los Angeles Public Library)

and said, 'Something has to be done about this smog, because it's ugly and unhealthy.' Our children couldn't even go out and play. That's when we started a group called 'Stamp Out Smog.'"

Marge Levee explained that they received public support by holding rallies and marches. Sometimes, they'd bring their children and have them wear gas masks. Newspapers and magazines wrote stories about the marches and printed pictures of people wearing masks, and pretty soon thousands of people wanted to join their group.

"Scientists told us cars and trucks were the biggest problem," she continued, "so we pressured government to make these vehicles cleaner. We were so popular that even the Governor met with us. We got Californians to write letters to elected state officials and help get a lot of new laws passed to clean the air."

"But it's still smoggy," Luna said.

"That's true," Marge Levee replied, "but we've only been at it for a few years. It's going to take many, many years, but our leaders finally seem to understand how important it is to clean our air." Mrs. Levee motioned toward Sabrina Schiller. "You kids should talk to her. She has a great idea for making even more progress in the fight against smog."

"Well," Mrs. Schiller said, "I'm a little sad today, because no one seems to like my plan."

"Would you tell the children a little more about that?" asked Mrs. Johnson.

"Sure," Sabrina Schiller said. "We know that all these

"Stamp Out Smog" sponsored "Share-a-Ride Day" to encourage people to cut back air pollution and traffic congestion by using buses and carpools to get to school and work.

cars and trucks on the road are making smog worse. And I'm worried that my husband, who is a TV writer, might get sick breathing all the bad air when he's stuck on the freeway going to and from work. What if we could take a lot of those cars off the road? Wouldn't that help? And it would make the freeways less crowded, too. So I came up with something called 'Share a Ride Day,' when people would carpool and ride buses. It was just a one-day experiment to see if people were interested."

Mrs. Schiller continued. "We had famous actors and actresses go on TV and urge people to get out of their cars. The city supplied lots of buses around town so people could take them to work. Newspapers, television and radio stations did stories about the experiment. And yesterday was the day."

"You said you were pretty sad. Didn't the experiment work?" Luna asked.

"No, it was a big flop. No one wanted to get out of their cars. At some bus centers no one showed up. Not one person! A total of six people rode the special buses, and four of them got on by mistake. The freeways were as crowded as ever with no evidence that anyone bothered to share a ride."

"It was a good try," Mrs. Levee said. "I guess if people don't want to get out of their cars, we'll just have to make the cars cleaner."

Mrs. Johnson then spoke up. "As you know, we've come here from the future."

"Of course," Mrs. Levee said.

Mrs. Johnson turned to Sabrina Schiller. "I know you're a little upset now, but I can tell you both that in the years ahead, your hard work will pay off. The sky will be less smoggy, and people will understand that carpooling can ease congestion and help clean the air at the same time. Just here in Los Angeles, there will be hundreds of special freeway lanes for carpoolers who share rides to work. And cities all over the country will have them. Not only that, a lot of cities will build special little railroads to take people to and from work so they won't have to use their cars all the time."

"Oh my!" Mrs. Schiller exclaimed. "You mean my experiment maybe wasn't a failure after all? I feel much better now. Thank you so much for telling me that."

Bobby interjected. "You know, Mrs. Johnson is right. My grandmother grew up in Los Angeles, and she says the smog used to be a whole lot worse. She tells me that before the new laws were passed—thanks to you—you couldn't even see the sky on many days, and the smog made her eyes water and her throat burn."

Marge Levee responded, "It's nice to know all our work will help the people live healthier lives in the future."

"One more thing," Mrs. Johnson said. "You don't know this, of course, but eventually experts in different parts of California will work together for cleaner air. And there will be a special group of people in charge—called the Air Resources Board. By the way, a woman—Mary Nichols—will lead that state board for many years."

"Very interesting," Marge Levee said. "Thanks for telling us this."

"Actually, it's *we* who should be thanking *you*—both of you, and all the women who helped you," Mrs. Johnson said. "You opened our eyes to how important it is to have clean air, and you pressured our leaders to do something about it."

How Women Saved San Francisco Bay

Back in 1961, three women who lived across the bay from San Francisco read a newspaper article about how fast the shoreline was being filled in by developers who wanted to build lots of homes and other buildings.

The women worried that they were losing the San Francisco Bay as a natural beauty and the home to much wildlife. They decided to do something about it.

The three women—Ester Gulick, Kay Kerr, and Sylvia McLaughlin—started an organization called "Save the Bay." They challenged wealthy landowners, powerful politicians, and big companies to stop building on the shoreline.

Their work resulted in a new state law to preserve the beauty of the bay.

Since then, "Save the Bay" has been a leader in protecting the environment of the San Francisco Bay Area and Northern California. It has worked hard to keep the water fresh and clean and to protect wetlands that support fish and wildlife habitats.

Over the years, thousands of volunteers planted more than 30,000 native plant species along the shoreline, and they made sure that trash was removed from the nearby roads before it could reach the bay.

7

Groundbreaking
Women of the '60s

Marina, Bobby, and Luna had just finished telling their fellow students about their exciting visit to the giant redwoods in far Northern California and to Los Angeles. Some of the students had heard about the smog problem, but none was aware of the effort to save the redwoods in the mountains and along the coast.

"We only have a few more trips planned," Mrs. Johnson told the class. "This next one should be pretty interesting, because it involves more women blazing trails at the Capitol. One person we'll visit was the first woman ever to win a California statewide election."

"Was she a Governor?" asked one student.

"No," Mrs. Johnson said. "But she did become State Treasurer, a very important job. We'll also be visiting two others who broke barriers in the State Legislature. So, who's going on this trip?"

Kayla, Jasmine, and Malik quickly raised their hands.

Mrs. Johnson said, "OK. If you're ready, let's go."

Once inside the time machine, Valerie went through her calculations. "I think you're going to enjoy this first stop," she told the students. "We're first going back to April 25, 1969, and if I'm right, the machine will take us exactly to the west steps of the State Capitol around noon."

In an instant, the children were back to an earlier era, and when they walked out of the time machine, they found themselves in the middle of a large crowd just outside the Capitol. Many of those gathered were holding signs.

"This looks exciting," Malik said. "I wonder what's going on. Can we stay and watch?"

Mrs. Johnson looked at her watch. "Yes, we're going to watch what's going to happen here. But first we're going to scoot into the Capitol, because we have an important appointment."

As the crowd continued to wander about, Mrs. Johnson hurried the kids through a large double door. They made their way to the Governor's office. She told the secretary at the front desk that the students from the future had arrived. The secretary pressed a buzzer, and within a few minutes, a woman led the students down one hallway, then another, until they came to a big meeting room where a man and a woman were ending their conversation.

"Hello and welcome. I'm Ronald Reagan, the Governor of California," the man said. "I know you're here to see the State Treasurer. We just finished a meeting, so she'll be with you in a second."

"Wow," Kayla said. "We know who you are. You used to be a movie star, and you become President of the United States in a few years."

The man laughed. "I did used to be in the movies, but I'm not thinking about being President right now, only Governor."

Kayla walked up to the man quickly and whispered into his ear, "You'll see."

76

Governor Reagan laughed again. He picked up a large bowl from his desk and asked, "Would you like some jelly beans?" Malik and Jasmine each took a small handful.

"Thank you," Kayla said, "but my mom doesn't like me to eat candy."

"Well," the Governor said, "I have to leave and give a speech across town, but I want you to know that we have a great Treasurer. I'm sure you'll have a nice conversation. Bye now."

As soon as the Governor left, Ivy Baker Priest, the first woman in California history to be elected to a statewide office, welcomed the children and told her story.

"My dad was a gold miner in Utah, but I was always interested in government. When Dwight D. Eisenhower ran for President in 1952, my job was to convince women to vote for him, so I traveled around the country talking to women's groups. After he became President, he appointed me U.S. Treasurer.

"What does the U.S. Treasurer do?" asked Kayla.

"One of the main jobs I had was being in charge of the U.S. Mint," Mrs. Priest said. "That is where all our money is printed."

She reached into her purse, pulled out a one-dollar bill, and pointed to the bottom left-hand corner. "That's my signature. It's on every bill that was printed when I was U.S. Treasurer.

Before Ivy Baker Priest was elected California Treasurer in 1966, she was the U.S. Treasurer. Her signature was on every dollar bill.

When I gave speeches, I used to joke: 'We women don't care too much about getting our pictures on money as long as we can get our hands on it.'"

"So, is your job as California Treasurer the same as it was when you were U.S. Treasurer?" Kayla asked.

"Actually, not at all," Mrs. Priest replied. "First of all, states don't print money. Only the U.S. government does that. One of my main jobs now is to take the money the state gets from taxes and invest it wisely."

"How does it feel being the first woman to win a state-wide election in California?" asked Malik.

Mrs. Priest smiled. "I'm very proud of that achievement. I won a close race a few years ago. I'm going to run again next year, and I think I'll win pretty easily."

A clock on the wall said it was two minutes after noon. Mrs. Johnson didn't want the children to be late for a special event outside the Capitol, so she thanked Mrs. Priest and took Kayla, Malik, and Jasmine back to the west steps of the building.

People were cheering and a band played an old song called "Brother Can You Spare a Dime." The children were spellbound as they watched a small Asian-American woman, wearing high heels and a nice business suit, pick up a heavy sledgehammer and smash a toilet to bits. As the crowd yelled, the students couldn't help but laugh.

"This is so cool," Malik said. News photographers snapped pictures to send around the world. TV crews gathered around to capture video. Reporters quickly scribbled notes for the stories they would write.

The woman, Assemblywoman March Fong, talked to some of the reporters, and then walked over to the students. "So nice to meet you," she said graciously. Kayla was the first to

March Fong, the first Asian-American woman elected to the State Assembly, smashes a toilet on the steps of the Capitol in 1969 to protest against women having to pay 10 cents to use many public restrooms.
(AP Photo/Walter Zeboski)

ask a question. "What was that all about? Why did you break that toilet?"

"Well," Mrs. Fong said, "you come from the future where life is different for women. But here in 1969, if a woman is out in public and needs to go to the bathroom, she has to carry a dime with her to unlock the bathroom stall in most public buildings. Sometimes I get so mad about it that I have one of my young children sneak into the ladies' room, crawl under a stall door and unlock it from the inside."

"You're kidding, aren't you?" asked Jasmine. "You have to pay to use the bathroom?"

"Yes, it's true," Mrs. Fong said. "And I think that's unfair to women. That's just one of many ways women are treated differently than men. I'm an Assemblywoman, and I'm trying to pass a law to change it."

Malik interjected, "So you thought that wrecking that toilet will help you change the law?"

"Well, look at all those news reporters," she said. "This story will be in newspapers and on TV and radio throughout California. I'm hoping women—and men—will see the stories and write angry letters to lawmakers about how women are treated unfairly. I think eventually we'll change the law—maybe not this year, but in the near future."

The Assemblywoman took the children and Mrs. Johnson into her office inside the Capitol where they continued their conversation.

"Is it true that your parents came to California from China?" asked Jasmine.

"Well, my mother did. My father was born in San Francisco. They owned a hand laundry in a small town in the San Joaquin Valley, and later, near San Francisco. They were very poor, and I realized how important it was to do well in school. I studied very hard and was a straight-A student in high school. I wanted to be a scientist, but I was told that because I was Chinese, nobody would ever hire me. I never forgot that."

"And in 1966, you became the first Asian-American woman to be elected to the State Legislature," Jasmine said.

"Yes, that's right. I didn't have much money or many people on my side at first, but my two children and I knocked on hundreds of doors and talked to thousands of voters in my district. It worked."

Mrs. Johnson then interrupted the conversation. "Assemblywoman Fong, if it's okay with you, we're going to go back into our time machine and return to see you again in 1994. Is that OK?"

"Oh my," Mrs. Fong said. "I can't help but wonder what the next 25 years have in store for me."

"Don't worry," said Mrs. Johnson. "You'll be even more famous than you are today."

With that, the students excused themselves and rushed out to Alberta. Valerie had been guarding it from curiosity seekers. They rushed inside and watched Valerie program Alberta's computer. When their time trip was over, they had been transported to February 16, 1994, a few blocks away from the Capitol—at the Secretary of State's office. They walked inside the building and saw an older version of March Fong packing up some boxes.

"Hello kids," the Secretary of State said. "it's nice to see you again after all these years. You haven't changed a bit, but a lot has happened to me since we last met. I got remarried, so now I'm known as March Fong Eu. And, back in 1974, I was elected Secretary of State by the voters of California—the first Asian-American woman in our nation's history to be elected to a statewide office. I was re-elected four times."

"What does the Secretary of State do?" asked Jasmine.

"That's a good question," Mrs. Eu responded. "The Secretary of State has a lot of duties, from being in charge of the California State Archives where all the government's historical records are stored, to many duties related to businesses. But the most visible and important one is being in charge of our elections. Over the years I've tried to make it easier for Californians to vote, to make sure they are better informed about candidates and ballot measures, and that everyone plays by the rules."

The Secretary of State paused for a second and remembered her last conversation with the students 25 years earlier.

March Fong Eu
Secretary of State Building

March 29, 1922-December 21, 2017

Dr. March Fong Eu was a trailblazer in California government and politics. During her 19 years as Secretary of State, she innovated voter registration by mail and the electronic reporting of election results. She streamlined business filings, enhanced the stature of the State Archives, and strengthened notary public laws and protections. Her leadership led to the construction of the Secretary of State Building now named in her honor.

She served in the State Assembly for 8 years, compiling an impressive record in education, public health and consumer protection. Dr. Eu was a forceful advocate for women and an inspirational voice for underrepresented communities. She was the first woman elected California Secretary of State and the first person of Chinese descent elected to a statewide office in the United States.

Dedicated March 25, 2019
Governor Gavin Newsom
Secretary of State Alex Padilla

A plaque at the Secretary of State building in Sacramento commemorates March Fong Eu's many accomplishments, including becoming the first female Secretary of State in California history. The building is named in her honor.

"Remember when I took that sledgehammer to the toilet?"

"Of course we do," Malik said. "That was the best part of our trip."

"Well, I wanted to strike a blow for women's equality back then, but the men in the Legislature weren't too happy with me, so the bill didn't pass. But I tried again and in 1974 we won."

"Hooray for the women!" shouted Kayla.

"So, why are you packing up all those boxes?" asked Jasmine.

"Well," Mrs. Eu said, "I'm changing jobs. President Bill Clinton has just appointed me to be Ambassador to Micronesia—which are hundreds of small islands in the Pacific Ocean near Australia. Tomorrow is my last day as Secretary of State, so

I'm packing up some of my things. It's been really great serving the people of California for 27 years, and it was so nice to meet you."

"This has been a fabulous experience for the students," Mrs. Johnson said. "But you look very busy. We're off now to visit Yvonne Brathwaite Burke."

"Oh, you'll like her," Mrs. Eu said. "We started in the Legislature together way back in 1966, and have remained good friends. She's had quite a career, too."

Kayla, Malik and Jasmine left the Secretary of State's office and walked to the time machine, which had become quite a curiosity as it sat a few blocks from the Capitol. People were trying to look inside, and there was even a TV cameraman taking pictures of the students as they walked into the machine and greeted Valerie.

"Where to now?" Malik asked excitedly.

"We're going to Los Angeles in 2004, where Mrs. Burke has spent many years on the Los Angeles Board of Supervisors," responded Mrs. Johnson.

In an instant, the visitors from the future were transported to a large meeting room in Los Angeles County's Hall of Administration Building. The room was empty except for one woman sitting at one end on a raised platform.

"I've been expecting you," she said.

"It's very nice to meet you, Supervisor Burke," said Mrs. Johnson. "We hope you're not too busy to spend a little time with us. We just came from an interview in Sacramento with Secretary of State March Fong Eu back in 1994. She said to tell you hello."

Yvonne Brathwaite Burke smiled. "That's great. March and I have been friends for nearly 40 years."

After the kids were offered cups of hot chocolate, they began their interview. Malik went first. "Do you often think about the fact that you were the very first African-American woman to be elected to the State Assembly?"

"I do," she said. "I was honored to win that election in 1966. And once I was in office, I focused on issues that were important to other African Americans and women—like civil rights, fair housing, consumer affairs and women's rights."

"Can you give us an example?" Kayla asked.

"Sure," Supervisor Burke said. "Back in the 1960s, women couldn't get credit cards in their own names—only in the names of their husbands. I worked to change that. Another example was a new law we passed that authorized child-care centers on college campuses. That made it easier for mothers with small children to go to college and improve their lives."

Kayla continued: "Did you have any problems because you were Black or because you were a woman?"

"Actually, I did have a few problems. After I moved to Sacramento, I had to get a judge to force a property owner to rent me an apartment. That was because I was Black. Also, I was the only woman on an important Assembly committee, and sometimes a few of the committee members would have lunch together at a private club a block from the Capitol. But that club wouldn't allow women, so I made sure we moved the luncheons."

Malik looked at his notes and asked, "Didn't you go to Congress in Washington, D.C., after that?"

"Yes," Mrs. Burke replied. "After six years as a member of the State Assembly, I won a seat in the U.S. House of Representatives in Washington, where I tried to get more money for schools, programs to help the poor and new laws that protected minorities from discrimination."

Then she laughed and said, "But do you know what I'm most remembered for back then?" The students shook their heads. "I was the first woman in history to have a baby while

Yvonne Brathwaite Burke, California's first Black female Assemblywoman and member of Congress.
(Collection of the United States House of Representatives)

serving in Congress. Our daughter Autumn was born my second year there. We appeared together on the cover of *Ebony* magazine. I think she might run for the State Assembly herself, when she's a few years older.

"And now I'm on the Los Angeles County Board of Supervisors, serving my local community. My decisions affect the schools, courts, roads and highways, mass transit and many areas that impact people's daily lives," Mrs. Burke said proudly.

Jasmine asked the final question before the children had to go back to the time machine. "And didn't you once run for Attorney General, California's top law enforcement officer?"

"Yes I did, back in 1978," Yvonne Burke said. "Never had a woman, nor an African American, been elected Attorney General. I campaigned hard, but lost. That was the first time in my long career that I was defeated in an election. But I proved that a woman could do all the things necessary to be a good candidate. I bet that one day—not too far in the future—California *will* have a Black woman as Attorney General."

"I think you're right," Mrs. Johnson said. "We have to get back to our time machine now, but we certainly thank you for giving us a few minutes of your time."

"My pleasure," Yvonne Brathwaite Burke said. "Have a safe trip home."

What Was the Equal Rights Amendment?

Many people don't realize it, but women and men in the United States are not guaranteed equal rights in the U.S. Constitution. And throughout history, women have been guaranteed fewer rights than men.

More than a century after the original U.S. Constitution was written, women finally were given the same rights as men when it comes to voting. After women won that national right to vote in 1920, they pushed for other rights that they believed they deserved, such as an end to discrimination in getting jobs and owning property. But they were unsuccessful.

Since then, a number of laws have been passed to give special protection to women in some areas, and similar rights and opportunities as men in other areas. Many women say they don't go far enough to make women the true equal of men. In addition, many individual states—like California—have given women equal rights. Still, many others have not.

That almost changed in the 1970s. Women activists fought hard to get an Equal Rights Amendment (ERA) approved by Congress. It was 24 words: "Equality of rights under the law shall not be denied or abridged by the United States or by any state on account of sex." But the federal rules said it needed 38 of the 50 states to vote to adopt it, and it fell three states short.

8

More Barriers Broken in the 1970s & 1980s

wo girls and a boy were huddled around a computer screen, taking notes, when the rest of their classmates came into the room just after the first bell rang.

"OK class, we're getting near the end of our adventures with Alberta, but we still have a few exciting discoveries to go," said Mrs. Johnson. "Today Taliesha, Maria, and Darnell will be going back to 1983, when some of your parents might have been very young—younger than you are now! Darnell, who will we be meeting with today?"

Darnell looked down at his paper before explaining. "We'll be visiting four leaders who helped bring a woman's point of view into the Legislature, where state laws are written. We'll also meet the first woman in California history to lead the State Supreme Court, where disagreements over those laws are settled," he said. "These women were trailblazers in the 1970s and 1980s. There were few women before them, but many more have come since."

"OK, so let's get going," said Mrs. Johnson.

Even though they had seen pictures and heard wonderful stories from their classmates who had already traveled

It was not until 1976 – 126 years after California became a state – that the State Senate had its first woman member – Rose Ann Vuich.
(California State Senate)

with Alberta, Darnell, Maria, and Taliesha still were amazed by what they saw when Valerie opened the door.

"Calm down and take your seats," said Mrs. Johnson.

"Here we go!" said Valerie. A few moments later, they were sitting in the visitor gallery high above the State Senate Chamber at the Capitol in Sacramento.

Mrs. Johnson pointed to a woman sitting at a desk in the middle of the large room below them. "That's Rose Ann Vuich, the first woman ever elected to the California Senate. Let's go down and meet her."

Senator Vuich walked out to greet them. She had a big smile and, in spite of her dark black hair, she looked like someone's grandmother. She carried a little porcelain bell. "Hello kids," she said. "What do you think of our new chambers? Well, not new, really, but completely reconstructed."

"It's beautiful," said Taliesha.

"Everything is so bright and shiny," added Darnell. "I like the red carpet."

Maria was anxious to hear more from the first Senator she had ever met. "Tell us about what it was like to come to the Senate."

"Ah, yes. You see, there never had been a woman in the California Senate before me," she began. "I was elected in 1976 —that's 126 years after California became a state—and the men didn't know how to treat a woman breaking into their club, so there were a lot of traditions and customs that had to be changed. For example, they usually began a speech saying 'Gentlemen of the Senate.' Obviously that didn't work with me, but it was a hard habit for them to break. So, every time they would say it, I would ring this little bell to remind them I was there, too!"

"Did they ever change?" asked Maria.

"It was hard for them, but yes, eventually. Especially when my colleague, Senator Diane Watson, was elected two years after me." Senator Vuich chuckled. "I was from a farming family in the Central Valley. She was from a big city, Los Angeles, but we quickly worked together to change things around here."

Just then, another woman came walking out of the Senate chamber toward them. "Here's Senator Watson now," said Senator Vuich.

"Hello, you must be the children who are doing the women's history project," said the Los Angeles Senator.

"That's us!" Taliesha responded proudly.

"Thank you for agreeing to meet with us," said Mrs. Johnson.

"Of course, I am proud to be part of California history," said Senator Watson. "I was the first Black woman ever elected to the State Senate."

In 1978, Diane Watson became the first Black woman to be elected to the State Senate. (California State Senate)

Remembering that he was there to do research, Darnell quickly jumped in and asked, "What kinds of challenges did you face in dealing with a Senate where there were so few women?"

The two women looked at each other and laughed. "Well, when I came here, the Capitol was being renovated," said Senator Vuich. "In the past, they only had a men's restroom and lounge for Senators in the historic Capitol—for the obvious reason. But when Senator Watson came to the Senate, they realized they were going to have to create one just for women."

Senator Watson jumped in and finished the story. "They did build us our own restroom and put a rose on the door. It's called the 'Rose Room,' honoring Rose Ann Vuich." Both women chuckled.

Taliesha wanted to know how it felt to be a Black woman coming in to a Senate that had seen few members of color since statehood in 1850.

"Well, several minority women had already served in the Assembly before I got here. There were March Fong and Yvonne Brathwaite in the sixties, and Teresa Hughes and

Maxine Waters—both African Americans from Los Angeles—in the mid-seventies," said Senator Watson. "And Gwen Moore, another African American, was elected to the Assembly in 1978, the same year I was elected to the Senate. So, the ground had been broken before I got here."

"Well, we've taken enough of your time, and we have a couple of more stops today," said Mrs. Johnson.

"Yes, thank you," chimed in the three young researchers, almost at the same time. And within moments they were in another room in the Capitol that was similar to the Senate Chamber, only larger and with beautiful green carpet.

"Wait here, I'll tell Assemblywoman Gloria Molina we've arrived," said Mrs. Johnson. The three kids looked around and noticed this wide hallway was much busier than in the Senate, with more people coming and going, more visitors, more everything. Above the two shiny, high wooden doors they saw the words: Assembly Chamber.

They knew from their research that the Legislature is made up of two bodies, or "houses"—the Senate and the Assembly. "When laws are created or changed, they have to be reviewed and approved by both houses and signed by the Governor," reminded Maria. "And with 80 elected members, the Assembly is twice as large as the Senate," added Darnell.

Just then Mrs. Johnson returned with a woman at her side. "Please say hello to Assemblywoman Gloria Molina," she said to the young students. They did politely, as requested. Maria realized that the woman looked much like her Aunt Elena. "I'll bet she's Latina, too," Maria thought.

Gloria Molina began her story: "My home is in southeast Los Angeles. When I was pretty young, I worked hard to improve the lives of Mexican-American girls and women. My parents wanted me to be like many of their friends—settle

Gloria Molina surprised the experts in 1982, when she became the first Latina to be elected to the California Assembly.
(County of Los Angeles/Diandra Jay)

down and marry someone and have tons of children.

"But, while I didn't have much confidence in myself, I really couldn't just stay home. I was committed to helping in my community. I jumped into politics, and I even worked for President Jimmy Carter in Washington, D.C. After that, I came back home to California, and a few people suggested that I run for the State Assembly."

"Wow, after working for the President, it must have been easy for you," said Maria.

"Well, it turned out to be very tough," the Assembly-woman replied. "A lot of people, even many of my friends, told me not to run. They said I couldn't win.

"But then something happened that changed every-thing," she continued. "A local newspaper reporter wrote a story that said I would probably lose because I'm a woman." Assem-blywoman Molina laughed out loud. "That was a big mistake.

I sent that story out to women's groups, women friends and others who were as upset as I was that someone would say a woman couldn't win. Those women sent thousands of dollars to help my campaign, and it worked. I won and taught a lesson to those who said I couldn't do it."

Maria smiled with shared satisfaction and looked at her notes. They reminded her that Ms. Molina would spend five years in the Assembly and sponsor laws important to women and children. One new law helped keep kids from dropping out of school. Another law helped protect girls and women from being bullied.

"You know," she told the students. "I really like working here at the Capitol, but I think in a few years I'm going to go back home so I can focus on helping my community."

"Thank you for your time," Maria finally said, clearly impressed, but aware that Mrs. Johnson was starting to look at her watch. "It's wonderful to hear stories like this from someone similar to me, who I can admire, who can be a role model for me. Thank you!"

They all said farewell and returned to Alberta for the final part of the day's journey. Just a few seconds later, they were in a San Francisco restaurant with a beautiful view of the waterfront and Bay Bridge. A woman sat at a table before them. They had been transported to November 10, 1986.

Mrs. Johnson introduced Rose Elizabeth Bird. "She was the first woman on the California Supreme Court and the state's first female Chief Justice," the teacher said. "That means she was in charge. As a result, people still call her 'Chief Justice Bird,' even though she's no longer on the court."

"Have you heard of the Supreme Court?" the Chief Justice asked.

"Yes we have," Darnell responded. "We learned that the

Governor Jerry Brown appointed Rose Bird to be California's first female Chief Justice of the California Supreme Court in 1977.

U.S. Supreme Court is the highest court in the country, and the California Supreme Court is the highest court in the state."

"That's right," she responded. "So, do you have any questions for me?"

"Sure do," said Taliesha, explaining that the class project was to learn about the important California women who have had little exposure in the history books, and to learn about the hurdles they faced. "As Chief Justice, did you have any challenges?"

"You've come to the right place with that question," the former Chief Justice answered. "I spent nine years on the court, and it was one big challenge for me." She laughed and added, "And I think it was a big challenge for a lot of Californians who didn't like me."

"Why didn't some people like you?" Taliesha asked.

"Well, I honestly think that some of them were uncomfortable seeing a woman Chief Justice." She went on to explain that she was appointed to the court by former Governor Jerry Brown, who wanted to bring more women and minorities into government, including the courts. "When I was on the court, we made a lot of changes that people didn't like. Many times we ruled in favor of prisoners and minorities, the poor and workers. That was a big change that people weren't used to."

She paused to let the students catch up taking notes. "I also must say that I thought many criminals—although they may have done bad things—were being punished too harshly. And that angered a lot of people, too."

"Our research showed you were voted out of office, along with two other male justices appointed by Governor Brown."

"That's right," Chief Justice Bird said. "That was just a few days ago."

"How did you deal with that?" Taliesha asked.

"On election night, I joked that I was taking it just like a man!" Chief Justice Bird said. "But it was a terrible disappointment, of course. It had never happened before. I really believe that as a woman, I was treated differently. But I also realize that my beliefs weren't the same as those of many Californians, that maybe I was trying to change our culture too quickly."

Mrs. Johnson stepped in and said it was getting late, and it was time to get back to school.

"Well, I think you're to be complimented on a wonderful history project," said the Chief Justice. "Thank you for including me."

"And thanks to you," said Darnell and Taliesha together.

"Your example of the challenges facing women was very enlightening," added Maria. "Thank you."

Valerie was waiting for them alongside Alberta. "Great!" she said. "You covered a lot of time today. Let's go home."

Oh My! A Woman Is Wearing Pants!

On a cold February morning in 1989, Becky Morgan became the first woman in history to wear pants to work in the California State Senate. The Senate, which saw no women members until 1976, had a formal dress code—coats and ties for men, skirts or dresses for women.

When Senator Morgan arrived for work, wearing wool slacks and a blazer, all eyes turned her way. "Hey, Becky's got pants on," one Senator whispered. A news reporter rushed to interview her. Articles ran in newspapers across America.

"What difference does it make who wears the pants?" Senator Morgan asked. She explained it was cold that morning and that she didn't like the new mini-skirt styles. "Frankly, the skirts now in fashion are shorter than I'm comfortable wearing."

Women had been challenging dress codes in America since 1850, when Amelia Bloomer invented a type of pants called "Bloomers." Back then, many women complained their dresses and tight-fitting corsets were uncomfortable. Bloomers allowed them to participate in sports and other active interests. In many places, however, it remained unacceptable for women to wear pants.

In 1960, the first women's jeans were introduced. In 1969, Charlotte Reid wore pants on the U.S. House of Representatives floor for the first time. That same year, Pat Nixon, President Richard Nixon's wife, was the first First Lady to wear pants in public.

9

Women Protest for Equality

As Mrs. Johnson's students began to file into the classroom on Monday, Zach, Stella, and Chloe were already there, preparing for the next adventure into the past with Alberta. Chloe pushed five sandwiches into plastic bags. Stella finished making notes from a page on the electronic tablet. Zach was putting away the broad paint brushes he had used to make a sign of some kind on a piece of cardboard. When the class had taken their seats, Mrs. Johnson asked Alka, sitting near the back of the room, to come up and join her.

"Everyone quiet please," she said, placing her hand on the girl's shoulder. Alka stared down at the floor, a sad look on her face. Chloe wondered what was going to happen next. Was her friend Alka in trouble?

"Class, I am happy that everyone in this room is very respectful of each other and looks out for one another," said Mrs. Johnson. "Sadly, that is not always the case in the world." She pulled Alka closer, wrapping an arm around the girl.

"This morning, two kids on the playground said mean things to Alka and made fun of her accent and dark skin. They told her she didn't belong here, that she should go back to where she came from."

A troubled murmur rose from the class. "Oh no," whispered Chloe.

"I've spoken with Alka's parents, and she's OK, but the words were very hurtful," Mrs. Johnson continued. "Unfair treatment like this is called discrimination and bullying. So today, let's show Alka that we don't discriminate here, and we are all her friends."

The room erupted in comments from Alka's classmates.

"That's horrible."

"Are you OK?"

"Don't be afraid, Alka, we're here for you."

"You're my friend, Alka."

Mrs. Johnson gave Alka a final squeeze. "Thank you. Let's be especially nice to each other today," the teacher said. Two girls near the front sprang from their seats and hugged Alka as she walked back to her own desk. Alka smiled for the first time, her embarrassment giving way to gratitude for her friends.

Mrs. Johnson held her palm high in the air and the class quieted down. "Stella, please fill the class in on the historic women the time travelers will be visiting today."

"We're going to be meeting with three women who were upset with what they saw happening around them and decided to do something about it," said Stella. "First is Felicitas Mendez, a mother who became angry when her children were told by the principal at their neighborhood school that they couldn't go there, just because they had dark skin."

Stella said that they would next visit Dolores Huerta. "She was concerned about the workers in our farm fields who faced some of the hardest living and working conditions of all. So, with a man named Cesar Chavez, she turned her efforts to bringing a better life to farm workers."

The last stop would be in Los Angeles to see Bobbi Fiedler, Stella said. "She was very upset that her children might not be able to go to their neighborhood school, too. We'll see how she won that battle."

Valerie was all ready to go when the three students and Mrs. Johnson arrived to board Alberta. "What the heck is that?" Valerie asked Zach, pointing at his hand-painted sign. "Stella and I learned that the women we're visiting today were all involved in social movements and that all of them at some point carried protest signs. I thought I'd bring one along and get their autographs on it."

"But they were involved in movements involving three different issues," Mrs. Johnson said. "How can one sign work for all of them?"

Zach held his sign up. It said "Respect Others. Do the Right Thing." He said he hoped they all would like it.

"I'm sure they will," the teacher said with a smile.

With that, Valerie entered some data on Alberta's keyboard, and in an instant they were in a place called Westminster, California, in 1954. A woman was sitting on a bench near an old run-down school that wasn't being used anymore. Next door was a very smelly cow pasture! Waving at a couple of flies buzzing near her head, she introduced herself as Felicitas Mendez and told them her story.

"Several years ago, back in 1943, I tried to send my three children to a really good school in our neighborhood. But the principal wouldn't admit them. He said they belonged in what he called a 'Mexican school,' the one that used to be here, next to this dairy farm. It was run-down and kind of dirty." Mrs. Mendez explained that sending her kids there was called "segregation," because the Mexican children were sent to a separate school from the modern schools the white children enjoyed. And treating them differently from other kids was called "discrimination."

"My husband and I thought that was unfair, so we went to court on behalf of 5,000 other Mexican-American children in this area to force the school district to allow us into the good schools. Some of the school officials told the judge these children with darker skin are not like other Americans. They need to go to their separate schools because they are inferior."

Stella, Chloe, and Zach looked at each other, remembering Alka's experience on the playground that morning. And they recalled how Mrs. Johnson also had used the term "discrimination."

"Our lawyers argued that the U.S. Constitution says all Americans are entitled to be treated equally. And the judge

Felicitas Mendez protested against discrimination in the 1940s when her children were banned from attending their neighborhood grammar school simply because they were Mexican Americans.

LOS ANGELES TIMES - FEBRUARY 19, 1946
RULING GIVES MEXICAN CHILDREN EQUAL RIGHTS

Felicitas Mendez and her husband won a major court victory in 1946, when a judge ruled that children couldn't be kept from going to their neighborhood schools just because of the color of their skin.

agreed, ordering the school districts in the area to end the segregation. And you know what?" Mrs. Mendez brightened. "This year, 1954, our case was the model for a U.S. Supreme Court case that ended official segregation of schools throughout the country. Now you and all your friends can attend school without being separated by the color of your skin."

Chloe thought about how unfair segregation was and wondered how it had ever been acceptable. Zach asked Mrs. Mendez to autograph his poster. And Stella closed her notebook, thanking Felicitas Mendez "for teaching us an important lesson."

"We've still got a lot of history to cover today," said Valerie. "Back to Alberta."

In an instant, they were sitting on the lawn in front of the California Capitol in Sacramento. It was summertime in 1972. A woman was speaking in front of a large crowd gathered facing the west steps. "We say you cannot close your eyes and your ears to us any longer! You cannot pretend that we do not exist!" she declared. "You cannot plead ignorance to our problems, because we are here."

In a few more minutes, that speaker was walking toward them, a smile on her face and her hand outstretched to Mrs.

Johnson. Their teacher introduced the three students to Dolores Huerta, who she said was a co-founder of the United Farm Workers of America. Ms. Huerta greeted the students warmly and revealed that she was mother to 11 of her own children and a mother figure for thousands of workers on California farms.

"When Cesar Chavez and I first started out, we wanted to make sure farm workers could live with respect, had decent housing, and got rest breaks while working in the hot fields," she explained. So they decided to form a union, which Ms. Huerta explained was a group of workers who join together to fight for better working conditions.

"We were determined to build a union to support them, not only winning higher pay and better working conditions, but also respect for the workers. That's what I mean when I say farm owners, elected officials, and others could no longer pretend we don't exist," she said.

"We had to be tough sometimes, and creative," Ms. Huerta concluded. "For example, when we had arguments with some farmers who grew grapes, we tried to convince people not to buy their grapes. It took many years, but it worked. This is called a boycott."

Dolores Huerta has fought for many years to improve the working conditions of California's farm workers.

More than 500,000 farm workers tend the fields in California.

Stella remembered reading that the farm workers' union was able to get growers to pay the farm workers more money and give them more breaks and restroom facilities.

Noticing how late it was getting, Valerie said the students needed to move on. Zach got his autograph and everyone not only thanked Ms. Huerta, but they also congratulated her on her success. And in no time, they found themselves outside a Los Angeles ice cream parlor. The date on Alberta's computer screen had said May 16, 1987.

"We're meeting Bobbi Fiedler here," Mrs. Johnson said. "We thought you might be ready for an afternoon snack." Inside, they immediately recognized her, because she was the one with the blouse with a big matching bow. Stella had read that bows were her favorite way to dress.

They all noticed that Ms. Fiedler was very soft-spoken.

**Bobbi Fiedler fought for voluntary busing and won election to the
Los Angeles City School Board**
(Bobbi Fiedler photo from the Collection of the Unites States
House of Representatives.)

But clearly her voice must have been loud enough to fire up thousands of parents and even teachers way back in the 1970s as she fought against rules requiring students to be bused across town as a way to reduce segregation in Los Angeles schools.

"We've learned that discrimination and segregation are horrible ways to treat people, especially children," said Chloe. "Why would you oppose something to get rid of segregation?"

Ms. Fiedler seemed to expect that question. "You see, parents were very angry that their children might be bused 35 miles or more from their homes," she said. "The whole idea of having neighborhood schools, the center of community life for many young families, was being destroyed," she added.

"But we realized that discrimination and segregation *were* unfair, too. So, we supported all kinds of voluntary plans and creative ideas that we felt would result in the same thing without ruining neighborhood life."

"What what were some of your ideas?" asked Zach.

"Well, we supported voluntary busing, for one thing," said Ms. Fiedler. "If some parents didn't mind sending their children far from home, that was OK with us. We also suggested such things as magnet schools. Those are schools with special programs where students would take extra classes in a foreign language, or math, or science. Those schools would be open to all students—even those outside their neighborhoods. We thought many parents would want to send their children to these schools."

Ms. Fiedler's approach won the support of hundreds of thousands of people, Mrs. Johnson pointed out. And within a year of starting her anti-busing campaign, Bobbi Fiedler surprised everybody by winning election to the Los Angeles School Board.

"Didn't you go to Congress, too?" asked Stella, remembering her research.

"Oh, yes, I was elected to the U.S. House of Representatives in 1980. At that time, I was the only woman in Congress from California," she said proudly. "I served six years and worked closely with President Ronald Reagan."

"Well, thank you for filling us in on your history, Ms. Fiedler," Stella said.

"And thanks for the autograph," added Zach. And as they headed for their return with Alberta, they looked back to see Bobbi Fiedler straighten her bow, smile, and wave goodbye to them.

Who Was Sylvia Siegel?

Every home needs energy for heat in the winter, air conditioning in the summer, and lights, computers, washing machines and TVs. Have you ever wondered where this energy—mostly in the form of electricity and gas—comes from?

Big companies, called utilities, provide most of the energy for California homes, and they are supposed to make sure that what their customers have to pay for it is fair.

In the early 1970s, Sylvia Siegel of San Francisco thought that these companies were charging homeowners too much money, and no one was asking them why. Even though she didn't know anything about these companies or the energy business, she decided to look into it.

Sylvia Siegel studied the companies that generated gas and electricity in California, and she found that they were charging higher rates for people in small homes and lower rates for companies that used a lot of energy. She thought that was unfair and backwards, and she started a group to fight the utilities.

Mrs. Siegel held protests demanding that the people's utility rates be lowered. Her small group grew to thousands of angry people. Many of them were poor and lived in small homes and could not afford high rates. Newspapers and television stations ran stories on these protests, and she forced the energy companies to lower their rates.

Over the years, Sylvia Siegel saved Californians billions of dollars in energy costs. Even when she was much older and had to live in a nursing home after breaking her hip, she was still leading protests, working to keep energy costs down for millions of Californians.

10

'Year of the Woman' and Beyond

M rs. Johnson waited for one last straggler to walk into the classroom. "Good morning, students," she said.

"Good morning, Mrs. Johnson," the class replied in unison.

"Well, today is our final trip in the time machine," Mrs. Johnson told the class. "Donald, Jack, and Stephanie will be visiting Washington, D.C., so they can interview Senator Dianne Feinstein. How many of you know who she is?"

About half the students raised their hands.

"I've seen her on TV," Lupe said.

"Me, too," said Eli. "She even ran for Governor many years ago. She didn't win, but she came pretty close."

"That's right. So, let me ask you another question," Mrs. Johnson said. "Since California became a state in 1850, how many women do you think have been elected Governor here?"

"Two?" replied Lucy.

"Three?" asked Thao.

Mrs. Johnson turned to Jack. "You've been studying about Dianne Feinstein in preparation for our trip. Do you know the answer?"

"Last week I wanted to be a nurse or a teacher. This week I decided to be a United States Senator. "
(Dennis Renault, *Sacramento Bee*, 1992)

"I sure do," he said. "It's zero. A woman has never been elected Governor of California."

"Good job, Jack," Mrs. Johnson said. "And we're also going to visit with another United States Senator from California—Barbara Boxer. This should be an exciting trip.

"One more thing," the teacher said. "I'm reminding everyone that once we return from Washington, I'm taking the entire class on a field trip to the State Capitol in Sacramento—by bus, not time travel. I have everyone's signed permission slip, so I think we're ready to go."

Mrs. Johnson, Donald, Jack, and Stephanie left the class in the capable hands of the substitute teacher and took their seats inside Alberta. Valerie made some calculations and programmed their trip: Constitution Avenue and First Street, N.E, Washington, D.C., January 5, 1993.

In an instant, they were transported 3,000 miles to the east. As they exited Alberta, the students and Mrs. Johnson were standing in front of the gigantic U.S. Capitol Building with its huge and distinctive dome. To their left, they could see the U.S. Supreme Court Building.

They were greeted by warm sunshine and a few puffy clouds in the sky. "My mom made me bring my heavy coat in case it snowed!" Stephanie said.

A woman overheard her, smiled and said, "Yeah, we call it shirt-sleeve weather. And starting today, a lot of women are going to be rolling up their sleeves to get to work."

Outside the Visitor Center, Senator Feinstein was waiting for them. "It's so very nice to meet you," she said. "Senator Boxer will be joining us a bit later."

"Not too much later, I hope," Donald said. "You know we can only stay one hour."

"That's OK," Senator Feinstein said. "We're on our way to meet her right now. Today is a big day in Washington, when all the new members of the House and Senate are being sworn into office."

"Then, how come you are out here with us?" Donald asked.

"Actually, I was sworn in a few months ago," she replied. "I won what is called a 'special election,' so I didn't have to wait to be sworn in like everyone else."

As they walked through the Capitol, Senator Feinstein told the children its construction had begun in 1793, when

Nancy Pelosi was first elected to the House of Representatives in 1987. In 2007, she was the first woman to be selected Speaker of the House. She became Speaker again in 2019.

George Washington was President. She said that it took many years to build and that the building was burned by the British during the War of 1812.

"We were lucky," she said. "A rainstorm helped put out the flames."

The Senator then took the children to the rotunda in the center of the Capitol, where they saw the large bronze statue of Ronald Reagan, who had been both a U.S. President and a California Governor.

Just then, a woman with long dark hair rushed past the students. "Hi, Dianne," the woman said. "I'm sorry I can't stop and talk. I'm late for a meeting before the swearing-in ceremonies."

"Kids, that was Nancy Pelosi. She was just elected to Congress a few years ago." Mrs. Johnson smiled. She turned to Senator Feinstein and said in a low voice, "You don't know this yet, but many, many years from now, she's going to become the first woman Speaker of the House." She then explained to the students that being Speaker meant that she would be in charge of the entire House of Representatives.

"My, that will be quite an honor," Senator Feinstein said. "Too bad she didn't have time to visit with us."

For a few moments, Senator Feinstein left Mrs. Johnson and the students in the upstairs gallery to watch her as she walked down to the Senate floor and escorted Barbara Boxer to the front so she could take the oath of office. There was loud applause afterwards. A few minutes later, the two women talked to news reporters. Senator Boxer, who was less than five feet tall, stood on a box next to Senator Feinstein as they were interviewed. Then, they joined the students to answer their questions.

Donald noticed that Senator Boxer looked like she was about to cry. "Is everything all right?" he asked.

"Actually, today is my mother's birthday," she said, holding back tears. "She died two years ago. She was Jewish and grew up in Austria, but her family didn't feel safe there. So, they came to this country before I was born. My life is the American dream."

Stephanie asked the Senators, "Why was 1992 called the 'Year of the Woman?'"

"Sure," Senator Feinstein said. "You know that over the years, men have always run our government," she said. "We've never had a woman President, and men have always been the leaders in Congress. But last year, a record number of women won election to the U.S. House of Representatives and the U.S. Senate."

"And look at the two of us," Senator Boxer said. "For the first time in history, one state—California—is entirely represented by two women in the United States Senate. And Illinois just elected the first African-American woman Senator in

In 1992, California became the first state to elect two women – Barbara Boxer and Dianne Feinstein – to the U.S. Senate at the same time.

history. It's pretty remarkable. Women are running for office—and winning—more than ever."

The two California Senators walked the students out the east side of the Capitol back to the time machine. They talked about their plans to protect the state's deserts, lakes and forests, and how they wanted California to have cleaner air and water and be a safer place for children and adults.

"This was really inspiring, even for a boy," Jack said with a smile.

"Yes," Stephanie added. "This was a great trip. I can't wait to tell everyone about it."

Once back in the classroom, Mrs. Johnson gathered the students and rushed them to a big yellow bus for the ride to Sacramento. On the drive, the students sang songs and discussed their trips on Alberta.

The bus parked in front of the Capitol, and the students walked through the security checkpoint. Mrs. Johnson had been to the Capitol many times and took them on a quick tour. She told them how the Capitol was built during the 1860s and that lawmakers first moved into the building in 1869. She showed them the old Governor's office that looked just like it did in the early days when Clara Foltz convinced the Governor to sign the bill allowing women to be attorneys.

The children admired the formal portraits of dozens of past Governors, such as Leland Stanford, Hiram Johnson, and Earl Warren. They particularly liked the entrance to the Governor's office, guarded by a sculpture of a large bear. Leading them down some long hallways, Mrs. Johnson pointed out dioramas set into the walls behind glass.

"There's one for each of California's 58 counties," she said. "Each one is supposed to tell its county's story."

"Look at Napa County," Vivian said. "It has pictures of beautiful vineyards and wine bottles." Humboldt County's diorama had pictures of a large forest, a river, and a beach. The students remembered the story about saving the forests there. Monterey's diorama showed images of agricultural fields that reminded them of Dolores Huerta, wine grapes, a golf course, a rodeo, a big bridge, and the famous Monterey Bay Aquarium.

Mrs. Johnson then took the class upstairs to the second floor. The students peeked into the back of the Senate, where a number of women and men were getting ready to have a large meeting that they called a floor session. Their last stop was a fancy office near the Senate. There to greet them was Toni Atkins, a State Senator from San Diego. "Welcome to Sacramento," she said with a warm smile.

On the bus ride, the students had learned all about Senator Atkins—how she grew up very poor in Virginia in a small

**Toni Atkins is the only woman to lead both the
State Assembly and State Senate.**
(California State Senate)

house that didn't even have an indoor bathroom. Her family didn't have enough money to take her to the doctor or dentist. The students also learned how she broke all sorts of barriers —becoming the first woman and first LGBTQ member to lead both the State Assembly and State Senate.

"I've been waiting my whole life to be a part of something that helps women be treated equally," she told them in a soft voice. She explained that she also wanted to help the poorest Californians find inexpensive places to live and get medical care if they are sick.

Senator Atkins explained that she couldn't talk for very long, because she was in charge of the Senate meeting that was about to start.

"That's OK," Mrs. Johnson said. "We have to get back home, anyway, because the students have a big writing project in front of them. You see, they have been going back in time to meet many famous California women who achieved so much during their lives, and they now have to write stories about them for our local newspaper. And they learned while we were in Sacramento that there is a rich treasure trove of California history in the State Archives if they need to research legislation or election results, state agency regulations and actions, census records or court cases."

On the bus trip back home, the students couldn't stop talking about their experiences. They were excited to finish their class project and write about the courageous and determined women they had met.

As the bus pulled into the school parking lot, Courtney stood in her seat near the back and said, "Mrs. Johnson, we want you to know that without a doubt this was the best school assignment we've ever had. Ever! Thank you for teaching us in such a fun way."

Modern Women Making California History

Most states have elected woman Governors. But, sadly, California has not. Meanwhile, one state—Arizona—has had four female Governors. The first woman Governor was Nellie Ross of Wyoming, who was elected in 1924.

California has an elected officer called Lieutenant Governor, who is the person who would run the state if the Governor dies or resigns. In 2018, 168 years after California became a state, voters elected their first female Lieutenant Governor, Eleni Kounalakis.

Eleni Kounalakis's family originally was from Greece. Her grandmother couldn't read or write. Her father came to California at the age of 14. He had no money and didn't speak English. He worked in the fields and as a waiter, went to college, and started a very successful home-building company. Lt. Governor Kounalakis worked at the company for 18 years, eventually becoming its president. Then, in 2010, President Barack Obama appointed her Ambassador to Hungary.

The Lt. Governor said she would like to see more women in leadership positions in California. In fact, two other California women won important elections in 2018—State Treasurer Fiona Ma and Controller Betty Yee. This was the first time in California history that three women were elected to statewide office at the same time—and there are only eight statewide offices. All three have said they might want to run for Governor some day. Maybe one of them will break our all-male record!

Key Dates for Women in California Politics

1850 – California becomes a state.

1878 – First woman practices law in California.

1896 – Suffrage vote for California women is defeated.

1900 – Federation of California Women's Club is formed.

1911 – Women win the right to vote in California.

1918 – First four women are elected to the California Assembly.

1923 – First California woman is elected to the U. S. House of Representatives.

1946 – An Orange County mother leads the fight that ends segregation in California schools.

1966 – First woman is elected to a California Constitutional office; minority women win seats in the State Assembly.

1972 – First California minority woman is elected to the U. S. House of Representatives.

1974 – First minority woman is elected to a California Constitutional office.

1976 – First woman is elected to the California State Senate.

1978 – First minority woman is elected to the California State Senate.

1992 – Two women are elected to the U.S. Senate, making California the first state to have two women serving in the Senate at the same time.

2007 – Californian becomes the first woman to serve as Speaker of the House of Representatives.

2018 – First woman is elected Senate President ProTempore of the California State Senate (previously she served as Speaker of the State Assembly).

2018 – For the first time in California history, three women are elected at the same time to constitutional offices, including the first female Lieutenant Governor.

2019 – A new record was set in the number of women serving in the California State Legislature.

A Few Words from Our First Female Archivist

Nancy Zimmelman Lenoil,
California State Archivist Emeritus

After the Gold Rush, and before California even became a state, it had a Legislature that made laws for the people to live by. On January 5, 1850, Governor Peter Burnett signed California's first law, which created the State Archives to keep and preserve the official records of the government. In the Archives are records of Governors and other constitutional officers, the Legislature, the state courts, as well as records of hundreds of individual state agencies.

The State Archives provides valuable information to people who want to learn about California's past. The earliest records are from when California was part of Spain and then Mexico, in the years before California officially became a state on September 9, 1850. The Archives includes millions of documents and books, 250,000 photographs, 20,000 maps and drawings, and more than 7,500 video and audio recordings. It also contains the records of virtually all of the elections since

California became a state, including the election of 1911 when California women won the right to vote, and 1918 when the first four women were elected to the State Assembly.

Many of the women who served in California state government have donated their records to the Archives, so future generations will know how women helped make California a better state. March Fong Eu, the first female Secretary of State in California and the first Asian-American to win a statewide office in the entire United States, is one of those women.

On March 6, 2006, I was proud to have been appointed the first female archivist in California history. As a child, I loved hearing stories about the past and my family's history. In college, I studied history and took classes on how to collect, manage and preserve historical documents for the future. For 13 years, I was honored to be able to lead the preservation and public sharing of thousands of records concerning the workings and decision-making of state officials and agencies, and especially highlighting the accomplishments of women officials. This is very important, because women who have contributed so much to California's history are often missing from the history books.

I encourage our younger generation to take a tour of the Archives or take advantage of its Research Room at the Secretary of State's office to learn more about California history and the women who made a difference in making our state a better place in which to live. In the same building as the Archives is the California Museum, and it proudly displays the stories of who and what formed this state. There is a permanent exhibit there about women trailblazers, as well.

**The State Archives and State Museum are located at
1020 O Street in Sacramento**

Getting to Know the Authors

Steve Swatt is a veteran political analyst and public affairs executive. He is a former award-winning political reporter with 25 years of journalism experience with the *San Francisco Examiner*, United Press International in Los Angeles, and KCRA-TV (NBC) in Sacramento. He received a BS in business administration and a master's degree in journalism, both from the University of California, Berkeley.

Susie Swatt is a former member of the National Advisory Council of the Institute of Government Studies at UC Berkeley. She spent nearly 40 years as a key staff member in the California Legislature. As a special assistant for the Fair Political Practices Commission, she researched and authored a study that won a national award for "investigative work in the public interest."

Jeff Raimundo spent more than 25 years as a political and public relations consultant based in Sacramento. Previously, he enjoyed a 25-year career as a newspaper reporter and editor with the *Sacramento Bee* and McClatchy Newspapers in Sacramento and Washington, D.C.

Jeff and Susie are members of the board of The Friends of California Achives.